TWO SPINSTERS AND AN ASSASSIN

TWO SPINSTERS AND A MURDER MYSTERY
BOOK 5

EVE TARRINGTON

To my mother, with love.

ALSO BY EVE TARRINGTON

Two Spinsters and a Corpse

Two Spinsters and a Duel

Two Spinsters and a Madman

Two Spinsters Books 1-3 Box Set

Two Spinsters and a Thief

Two Spinsters and a Villain (Coming Soon)

1

"Seasickness would have been a blessing," said Miss Judith St Clair delicately, taking a seat near the warmest fire she could find in the narrow, elegant residence. Outside, more snow drifted down the colourful streets of St Petersburg, the Russian winter as fierce and unrelenting as she had feared.

The gentleman standing in front of Judith frowned, and she wondered how to continue without offending him. She explained that their ship was so uncomfortable she'd wished for anything to occupy her mind, even illness. Some of the men had been so sick that they'd ended up on the decks, pouring out their souls, hoping in vain for the day when their stomachs would grow accustomed to the strange swaying of the ship.

For Judith, there had been nothing to distract from the small quarters, from the awkwardness of sharing every single space with hardworking men who were not supposed to speak with the lady passengers.

"It was worse than being confined in a carriage," Judith

said. "I'm afraid I could never love a ship unless it were a very grand one."

Judith could not bring herself to address the man before her as Monsieur Zharkov. It seemed an unthinkable liberty, though the Russians insisted it was quite correct. She was already blushing for reasons she would have had trouble explaining. So, instead, she called him "Monsieur Zharkov." After all, French was the language he had chosen as he spoke in loving tones of the Russian navy.

"I have never in my life seen a ship I did not love," he said. "I tell you, it is madness for me to walk past our harbors every day that I must be confined to land!"

Monsieur Zharkov took a chair next to Judith's. He was hardly taller than she was, with skin darkened by the sun and hair as black as any she had ever seen. His entire body seemed to be thick and strong, and she would not have been surprised to learn that he weighed at least twice what she did. It was rather strange for Judith, for when she faced him, his piercing eyes were exactly at the level of her own.

She attempted to stop thinking of his appearance. After all, she was an engaged woman, and at only twenty-six years of age, Monsieur Zharkov was hardly more than a child, or so he seemed to Judith. Though he might be of an age to marry a very young woman, surely, she was too old to interest him! In spite of the very great warmth of his gaze, his eyes never leaving her for a moment, Judith told herself that he was all politeness. He could not possibly be enraptured by an old spinster such as herself.

"Our ship was very small," she managed to say. "I never grew used to simply drawing a curtain at night rather than closing a door."

"Of course, and think of it without curtains! There is scarce space for all the men to sleep, even when we are on watch at all hours," he said, gesticulating with his hands as he spoke as if he were a hot-blooded gentleman from Tuscany. "But the ocean, I tell you! When we are in the midst of such vastness, what is a sleeping space?"

Judith blushed again. She had spoken with many people about their sleeping quarters, but something about her present conversation felt less innocent. True, Monsieur Zharkov had not said anything improper, but he was leaning so close to her that she felt he was practically inviting her to take another voyage.

Judith leaned back. "Thank you, no," she said. "I suppose we shall take another ship when we leave St Petersburg, but after that, I intend to be a land dweller."

"To be sure," said Monsieur Zharkov, "there are many great adventures to be had on land! You cannot think of leaving before the summer, surely? The ice has trapped us for only two months so far, and yet already, I am dreaming of our next voyage."

"I am not entirely sure," said Judith. "Yes, perhaps the summer."

Judith glanced at her friend, Louisa-Margaretta Haddington. Louisa-Margaretta, the daughter of a wealthy and prominent English family, had told Judith two months earlier that she was going to face an unpleasant punishment for her brief dalliance with a married man. Judith St Clair, a pious rector's daughter who had never thought she could condone Louisa-Margaretta's reckless behavior, felt for her dear friend. She'd begged the assistance of a painter whom they had befriended. Madame Chatel, who had survived a revolution while supporting herself as a portraitist, promptly took them to St Petersburg, where she and her grown daughter had been invited to spend the winter with English friends. Madame Chatel stated plainly that she would only be easy in a place where the odious Napoleon had already invaded and been repulsed and that she would throw herself under the protection of Emperor Alexander. In spite of her daughter's assurance that the English were more than prepared to fight off any future French invasions and that the imprisoned Napoleon Bonaparte was hardly likely to escape the isle of Elba and attempt another conquest of Europe, Madame Chatel insisted on living and working in St Petersburg.

It was a rich city, and Judith easily understood why the Russian winter had defeated the French invaders. Madame Chatel had sound financial reasons for settling there, as the wealthy families seemed intent on spending their money quickly and lavishly. Even the event they were attending, a soiree at the Prussian ambassadors' home intended to honor their native Christmas traditions, was one of the most opulent that Judith had ever seen. The decorations were fresh and beautiful, with scented boughs on all of the glistening surfaces, and even her best gown made her feel dowdy next to the elegantly dressed Russian, French, and Prussian ladies.

Louisa-Margaretta, of course, looked quite beautiful in her finery, though the green gown that she had chosen had needed to be taken in earlier in the day. Louisa-Margaretta's acquaintance with her married paramour had begun in September, and Judith knew that in the first few months, it was not uncommon for women to grow sickly and thin before their bellies began to grow large and round. Even so, she worried for her friend. They had discussed how to get Louisa-Margaretta to an appropriately discreet location in the Russian countryside once it was no longer possible to hide the approach of her confinement. They might attempt this in May or June. Then, after Louisa-Margaretta had recovered for some weeks, they would take advantage of the brief absence of ice to return to England by ship.

But the plan was going rather too well for Judith's liking. Louisa-Margaretta should have gotten at least a little bit stouter. Instead, though she continued to complain of feeling ill and tired, she looked much too thin. In addition, Louisa-Margaretta had been listless on the voyage and claimed that she was bored with their life in Petersburg, though she usually would have enjoyed the adventure. She had no interest in attending parties, learning Russian, or even going for rides in the grand carriage kept by their hosts.

At the moment, Louisa-Margaretta was stifling a yawn, and Judith could see that she was making only desultory conversation, though the group of ladies that included her was speaking French. A great deal of fuss had been made about the presence of three of the Emperor's many brothers and sisters, and Louisa-Margaretta could have conversed with the young and beautiful Anna Pavlovna. But even a princess could not rouse Louisa-Margaretta from the stupor that had been overcoming her for months.

"Let us take a pleasure boat out, then," said Monsieur Zharkov, his earnest face turned once again towards Judith. "In the spring, as soon as the ice has broken."

Judith tried not to think of spring. How would she explain her desire to go into the Russian countryside? Thus far, in between conversations with the ambassadors' friends in French and German, she had tried to learn Russian. Her pronunciation was good, but her grammar was a terrible mess. If she needed to communicate something urgently when Louisa-Margaretta's time came, she was not certain she would be able to do it.

"I'm afraid boats give me little pleasure," she said, trying to make her tone firm enough that the gentleman would take the hint. But he only nodded.

"Tell me what does bring you pleasure, then, mademoiselle. I can see that it is not grand parties. You and your companions seem heartily bored with this one."

Judith hastened to correct him. "I am sure we are not, and I am very sorry if we have given that impression. Indeed—"

"Indeed, you are, and who could blame you! I love parties myself, but it is much better if there is dancing. You must be a dancer, surely?"

Judith, who was not a dancer, feared that her answer might be construed as rude. "Well, I do love music. But more as a listener. I am not fond of dancing."

He leapt to his feet with the air of a puppy too long confined to a cage. "That is perfect! Here, we have a Frenchman who has been longing for the opportunity to exhibit. It is Ivo Solier, the finest little opera man I have ever known!"

He corralled a handsome gentleman who had been standing at the window, sulking, and brought him to Judith. She hoped that the gentleman had not heard that moniker "opera man," as it sounded rather like an insult. She hoped it was due only to the Russian gentleman's poor command of French, not some desire to insult Monsieur Solier's profession.

After the introductions were made, Judith forced a smile. "I am very interested in hearing about your work, Monsieur Solier."

"There is nothing to tell," the gentleman said sharply. Judith noticed that his face was rather handsome except for his dark expression, though this did not cause her any discomfort. Vain men never captivated Judith, and Monsieur

Solier was clearly above his company. Judith could tell that he took no notice of her.

"Pardon?" she said.

"I do not like to speak of my work," he said, speaking rapid French. "I can only show it. Do you play, then, Mademoiselle...?"

Judith could tell that he had not bothered to learn her name. And he was not trying hard to disguise that fact.

"I play," she said. "And I sing, passably. About a year ago, I had an occasion to learn a great deal of Bach, because I—"

But before she could tell the story of how she had become ever more enchanted with the work of her favorite composer, the man shook his head.

"I will play myself," he said. "It is my own work; there is no one better. Maxim, bring me a better singer than this woman."

Judith bristled inwardly, though she was too well-bred to show her annoyance. She had merely used the correct degree of modesty when speaking of her accomplishments. In fact, she excelled at the pianoforte. Her singing, while not as varied as a virtuoso's, was also much admired. But instead of trying to correct Monsieur Solier, she recommended her friend.

"Mademoiselle Louisa-Margaretta Haddington is an accomplished singer," she said. "She is my friend in the green dress, just there. If you would like a soprano, you need only provide her with music."

Monsieur Zharkov, who had already been introduced to Louisa-Margaretta, drew her away from her group and over to the pianoforte, where she stood leaning against the instrument as if she might fall asleep in that spot. He introduced her to Monsieur Solier, who had brought over a folio stuffed with papers and was pulling several out so quickly that he must have some system for keeping them all in order.

"I hope you sing well," he snapped, without looking at Louisa-Margaretta. "My compositions are not well-suited to amateurs."

ChapterBreak

Louisa-Margaretta, for the first time in many weeks, felt herself springing to life. She was often fatigued by the things others said to her, but on hearing the French composer's words, she felt a rush of a more familiar emotion. Rage threatened to overcome her, and she stood tall.

"I am only an amateur because nobody has ever paid to hear me sing," she said. "That does not mean I am not equal, or perhaps superior, to many of the women who are hired to sing your songs on the stage."

Mr Solier looked at her as if for the first time. He continued to speak French, but he plainly understood at least some of Louisa-Margaretta's words. "You would not wish to sing on a stage, then?"

"Certainly not. I am far too rich."

They appeared to be destined to trade barbs in their own languages. Louisa-Margaretta was not about to use French with this arrogant man, and he showed no inclination to speak English with her. But she was surprised to see him smiling.

"Rich, eh?" he said. "Well, well. I could use another patroness."

"Save your breath," Louisa-Margaretta said. "I have no intention of giving you money. But I will sing this aria that you have written out with such an inelegant hand, though I can scarce make out half the words. Consider that a gift."

He laughed, which then set off the large young man

standing next to Judith. "Monsieur Solier, I have never heard you laugh before! How fortunate we are."

"Get back," said the composer brusquely, all seriousness again. "Mademoiselle, er—"

"Miss Haddington," said Louisa-Margaretta in English. She much preferred to speak English, though her months with Madame Chatel had given her some facility with French. "My name is Miss Haddington, and it is not a difficult one. If you cannot bother to learn it, I shall not bother to address you as Monsieur Solier."

"Miss Haddington," Solier said. "You are ready?"

"Yes," said Louisa-Margaretta.

She had often heard stories about women singing when they were with child. Some said that the broad changes in one's body were detrimental to the voice, others that they added a mysterious and desirable quality to the music. This gave her a small sense of nervousness, but as she sang, it fell away. The aria, in fact, was not difficult. The harmonies that Monsieur Solier had chosen were strange, to be sure, but the part he had written was well within her range.

By the time she was halfway through the aria, she had noticed a shift in the room. In an instant, the entire company seemed to be around her, dozens of faces and glistening gowns shining in the candlelight as the guests competed for the best view.

2

____

J udith could hardly have believed it. The entire company was now crowding into the room with the pianoforte, and she could see that any young lady determined to demonstrate her own skill at that instrument would be cowed by the gentleman who was bent over it. To Judith's astonishment, Louisa-Margaretta was smiling. She and the French composer were taking turns leading. Louisa-Margaretta would grow faster or louder, then Monsieur Solier would add in an ornamentation or exaggerated dynamic. For the first time in many months, Judith's friend looked as if she were ready to laugh.

"Encore!" was the cry when Louisa-Margaretta finished singing the last aria he had laid before her.

As the composer attempted to look for another paper, Louisa-Margaretta stopped him. "'_Morirò, ma vendicata,_'" she said.

"Handel," sneered Monsieur Solier. "My arias are better than his. Every melody that man writes is forgettable."

"You dream of composing better arias than he does,

perhaps," said Louisa-Margaretta with a smug smile, to the general amusement of the company. "Play it."

Monsieur Solier, to his credit, played it well. It turned out that he was extremely accomplished on the pianoforte. Judith wondered aloud whether his performance was due to excellent memory or a secret love for George Friedrich Handel's work. And she was amused to watch her friend as Medea, hurling curses at the assembled company. If any of them knew how truly Louisa-Margaretta could embody that character, no doubt they would not find her quite so charming.

Monsieur Zharkov, however, shook his head before the performance was halfway through. "This room is too warm," he said. "We should eat something. I hate how late they serve meals at these gatherings. A man could starve waiting."

Judith had no wish to be drawn away from her friend, who was much more animated than she had been in weeks. "Perhaps after this next aria," she said, but Monsieur Zharkov had already offered his arm. Judith's words deserted her when she was faced with the prospect of refusing it.

And so they found themselves in the front room of the stately home, alone but for the servants and one young woman who was touching her carefully arranged curls rather more than she ought. Monsieur Zharkov had piled a plate high with all of the Prussian delicacies that had been left on a table in the adjoining room, and he was eating meat and dark bread with a gusto that showed he had been quite honest about his appetite. According to the way Judith had been raised, she and the other young woman ought not to have been left without a chaperone, though it seemed that these strictures were rather looser in St Petersburg than they had been in England.

Silently, Judith mused that she and the young woman ought to stay together in case they exposed themselves to comment or criticism. She decided to engage the young woman in conversation so as to keep her in the room. All it took was two young ladies rather than one to extinguish the tide of gossip.

"Was the music rather loud for you?" Judith said in French to the lady.

The young woman's eyebrows went up, and she said some words that sounded like very accented French or perhaps another language. She added her name, Mademoiselle Lara Claudio.

In England, it would not have been proper for them to converse without an introduction. But the young lady looked as if she were anxious for Judith to finish the ritual.

"Judith St Clair," she said. "And this is Monsieur Zharkov." Judith hoped that the young woman had not been long enough in Russia to demand the first name and patronymic, for introducing her companion as "Monsieur Zharkov" would have felt terribly forward.

"I hope you enjoyed the music too," said Miss Claudio quickly, not exactly answering Judith's question and continuing to look round.

"Yes." Judith could think of no other response. "I thought it was beautiful, so lovely that even the tables full of food were abandoned."

Monsieur Zharkov, who had worked his way through his portion, nodded. "Yes! They leave the meat, and even the fruit from the orangery, all to listen to some Italian nonsense. I couldn't understand more than every few words of what she was singing, your friend."

Judith permitted herself a small smile. Though Zharkov's French was fluent, by his own admission, it was because the language had been beaten into him. She could well believe that his Italian was not up to the task.

"In the aria Louisa-Margaretta chose, Medea is insulting all who have wronged her," said Judith. "Presumably, as a powerful sorceress, her threats of revenge carry some weight."

"Hmm," said Monsieur Zharkov. "Medea does not sound like a very agreeable lady."

"Well, perhaps you are right." Something possessed Judith to keep speaking, perhaps her knowledge of the many ladies she had met who could not have been described as "agreeable" but had gifts all their own. "Medea has indeed been wronged. But her determination in not simply accepting those wrongs but in fighting for justice, is that not something to admire? When a man seeks revenge for a great injustice, we call him honourable, and yet a woman performing the same acts is referred to as some sort of wild heathen."

The young woman, Miss Claudio, nearly jumped. Judith realised that perhaps the bloodthirsty Medea did not make a suitable topic for a polite gathering after all.

"Shall we go and listen to my friend once again?" she asked. "Miss Claudio, will you join us?"

The young woman coloured, shaking her head. "No. That is... Not at the moment."

She looked out the window then at Judith. It seemed as if she wished very much to leave the gathering. Perhaps Miss Claudio thought that Judith wished to be alone with Monsieur Zharkov. And it would not have been an unreasonable assumption, as they had left the performance alone. Or rather, not quite alone, but in only each other's company.

Judith resolved not be near Monsieur Zharkov again without another lady present, which meant that they could not walk back together to hear Louisa-Margaretta sing. Some people might assume that they had been alone, and tongues would certainly wag. Instead, they would need to stay in the front of the house, with its tall windows overlooking one of St Petersburg's many canals, which was full of ice and snow. The darkness had descended in the early afternoon, and Judith wished that the horrid weather would dim some of the enthusiasm of the revelers. Instead, she feared the gathering might last well into the night.

With a sigh, she glanced at the roaring fire. Monsieur Zharkov was on his feet, examining what Judith hoped was a ceremonial sword on the wall.

"This is damned impractical," he said then raised his eyebrows in surprise. "*Terribly* impractical—I apologise, ladies. Forgot my company for a moment!"

Judith, who had been easy with him a moment earlier, could now only manage a strained smile. She wasn't sure if Miss Claudio had mistaken them for a couple, but without asking directly, Judith could only do her very best to dispel that impression.

Just as she was wondering whether she ought to have told Zharkov not to take the sword down from the wall and make feints with it, behavior that would have gotten him thrown out of any proper English drawing room, a pale young man went quickly through the room. Judith would have been able to tell from the man's clothing that he was rich, but she would not have recognized him as royal if Monsieur Zharkov did not remark upon it.

"Where are you off to, then?" Monsieur Zharkov asked, but the man had gone.

Zharkov shook his head. "Awfully cold night to walk

back to the palace. I could manage it, but a thin child such as that one had better not try. There are many who will be very displeased with him, though I understand that a young man needs fresh air and exercise. I need it myself!"

Miss Claudio only looked away, but Judith gasped. "That was one of the princes?"

"Yes, the young one, Mikhail Pavlovich. Poor thing, his grandmama may have thought he had promise, but I'm sure parties like this are devilish dull for him."

"He really looked very ill," said Judith. "And is it wise for him to go out alone at night?"

"In this country, princes may do as they please," said Miss Claudio, one of her first contributions to the conversation. "Miss St Clair, what brings you to St Petersburg?"

Judith realised that she had been uncommonly rude with the young lady, forgetting to ask Miss Claudio about her own visit. Once more, she reflected that she was not showing her usual degree of courtesy or tact. It would have been convenient to blame Louisa-Margaretta, whose delicate situation was the reason for much of Judith's unrest, but she knew that her own mind had hardly been steady. She worried about her family, her fiancé, and the life in Derbyshire that she had once again abandoned. She dreamed of sailing away from Russia, into a future that would not be filled with so much doubt and bewilderment. But ever since they had landed in St Petersburg, the frost and the darkness had obscured her vision. She could not think of the future as easily as she once had, and she felt suspended, like her friend. Judith was left wondering if, after all her own dithering, Morgan Ramsbury had changed his mind and decided not to marry her. She was used to spinsterhood, but she was not at all used to the prospect of not marrying Morgan. In fact, every facet of her being rebelled against it.

She endeavored to calm both her breathing and her heart. Morgan had met Madame Chatel and realized that her way of thinking was becoming all too common in England. For the painter, perhaps it was understandable that she reject not only Napoleon Bonaparte but all of the reforms he had brought to France. Many of the Russians that Judith had met had similarly bitter views of that man, and as he had gone so far as to invade and burn down their capital city of Moscow, perhaps those views were justified. But both Morgan and Judith privately felt that all Europe was in danger of throwing the baby out with the bathwater. If a solution were not found for new alliances and borders, they would end up with the same sort of unequal, destabilised norms that had caused the wars in the first place.

For this reason, Morgan had decided to change his life and become a diplomat, a decision that Judith had heartily supported, though it necessitated a long engagement. In fact, at first, the length of her engagement was something of a relief, as she had initially kept her understanding with Morgan secret even from her family. She knew that they might well need some time to adjust to the idea of her marrying a Nonconformist, and she felt that she could bear the wait. But as the months passed and she heard nothing, she began to wonder if Vienna had changed Morgan's heart. He had decided to go there as a fledgling diplomat, helping to create a more just future for Europe, but the rumours of the other diplomats' wild parties and scandalous love affairs did nothing to still the doubts in Judith's mind.

Miss Claudio was plainly awaiting a response, and Judith shifted in her seat. "Madame Chatel, the painter, is a friend of our family. My friend Louisa-Margaretta Haddington and I wished to accompany her here to St Petersburg to see the city. We had never been abroad, and our families were only easy with such a proper situation, with a steady friend and an English family."

In fact, this was a lie. Judith's family had not been at all easy with the arrangement, but in spite of all the lies she had told about Morgan, she knew that her father still trusted her to keep her head. If her mother had been alive, Judith might not have been permitted to go. Mama would have seen through her feeble reasoning and gotten at the heart of the matter. Louisa-Margaretta's family did not approve in the slightest, but they could hardly refuse when she insisted. The stain of their decision to remove her from her beloved, Isaac, still clung to all of their choices.

"What brings you to St Petersburg, Miss Claudio?" Judith asked, remembering her manners once again.

But the young lady only shook her head. "My cousin," she managed to say. "She had business here, or rather friends. You see, our path is a sort of spiritual one."

Perhaps Miss Claudio became conscious of Monsieur Zharkov shaking his head. With a quick look away, she retreated into herself again.

"I'm sorry, I can't abide any of it," said the young man, shaking his head. "Statues crying? Books about prayers instead of action? Call me old-fashioned, but I have to respond to what I see before me, you understand? In the navy—"

Before the young man could start telling war stories to a young and sleepy audience, every bit as insensible of their desires as an old seafarer, they heard a shout from outside.

Judith rushed out, as did Monsieur Zharkov and the

young woman. More than enough light shone from the houses to see a young man on the bridge, shouting in Russian. Monsieur Zharkov ran over to him.

"It's Mikhail Pavlovich," he shouted back to Judith in French. "He went over the bridge. Get help!"

In England, Judith would have stayed, trying to get to the bridge and help the man herself. Though she hated swimming, she had been forced to learn from a young age. Her brothers, energetic and careless, might have drowned in a pond on many occasions if Miriam, Judith, and the other village children had not been skilled enough to save them. They were forever jumping in, getting themselves cold and muddy, then crying for help when it was time to get out.

But in Russia, Judith felt that her skin was burning in the cold, and she grabbed the hand of Miss Claudio. Tears stood in the young woman's eyes, and solicitude for her helped Judith remember her duty.

"Come in," she said to her. For Monsieur Zharkov had just jumped over the side of one of the canals himself, using a large bank of snow to cushion his fall. Judith took a better look at the canal and realized that the young prince had not fallen through but was on top of the snow. For the moment, the ice was holding. If they did not find assistance for the prince and Monsieur Zharkov, Judith knew that more than one man would run the risk of perishing.

As soon as they entered the house, the French words sprang to her lips as well as the Russian one which she had heard the young man yelling from the bridge.

"*Au secours! Pomogite!*" she cried over the roar of the music from the far room.

Though Judith would not have expected anyone to take note right away, the singing stopped. The pianoforte continued, but Louisa-Margaretta's commanding speaking voice came to the fore.

"Help for my friend," she said, her voice as loud as it was imperious. "At once!"

                                    3

                            ____

"You're sure you didn't see anyone else, Judith?" said Louisa-Margaretta. "It really seems most unlikely. Why were there not tigers in the front, holding the horses? Or some other servants, laughing and smoking? In London, there would have been a thousand witnesses."

They were having a quiet meal at the residence of the English Cluetts, their hosts in St Petersburg, but Louisa-Margaretta was alight with the thrills of the previous evening. Judith had begun to describe her experiences to the Cluetts, but she decided to let the subject rest.

"Ladies, please," said Susannah Cluett, the ambassador's wife. She looked as if she were about to faint into her soup. The Cluetts, like many diplomats, had an independent income that stretched to such luxuries as a French cook. Unfortunately, the cook had given notice as soon as the worst of the dark winter was upon them, and now, they were all making do with Russian cuisine. The cabbage soup, which Judith privately considered rather delicious, repelled the gentle Mrs Cluett. She had confessed that she preferred bland English offerings to the rich French food that their former chef had prepared, but she certainly did not consider Russian soups to be an improvement on their previous situation.

"One ought not to talk of such things," mumbled the ambassador, taking several large mouthfuls of soup while shaking his head. He puckered his lips, perhaps at the amount of dill floating in the thin broth, but he continued to eat nonetheless.

"We all felt how cold it was," Judith said, firmly enough that she hoped this answer would force her friend to abandon the subject. "In Russia, everyone takes shelter indoors but the horses, at least until it is time to leave. The manservant who saw the young man fall only did so because he had been sent from one house to another with a message."

Louisa-Margaretta let out a great sigh. After the excitement of the previous evening, she seemed livelier but tetchy. It was as if she had remembered how much enjoyment there was to be had in life and now resented that she was not being given her due.

Judith glanced around for Madame Chatel, who was often the voice of reason in a conversation such as this, but the painter was working. She had gotten a new commission and had stated that she was not to be disturbed. Of course, for Madame Chatel, work seemed to serve the purpose of a gentlewoman's "sick headache." It was a very convenient excuse for absenting herself whenever it suited her, especially if she felt that one of the young ladies was being rather too dramatic. Madame Chatel, having known danger and bloodshed, had no patience for the foibles of young people. Unfortunately, this included her own daughter, who often lamented that her mama did not wish to hear about any of her plans or feelings.

"Louisa-Margaretta," said Judith, "perhaps it is true that further discussion would be morbid."

"The thing is funny, not morbid," said Louisa-Margaretta. "Anyone trying to kill a Russian princeling ought to have known that the canals ice over in the winter. If one is to drown, there must be a terrifically deep hole in the ice. In fact, the canal is so shallow that I'm not sure there would be enough water to drown in. Though if we were to go back, perhaps, to see for ourselves—"

"I'm sure nobody was trying to kill him," said Judith hastily.

Louisa-Margaretta raised her eyebrows. "Honestly, Judith. You would suppose that someone was simply trying to throw him into the canal as a sort of joke? Has he told us anything more of his attacker? I heard that he claims he cannot identify the figure who pushed him. Of course, he refuses to say why he left the soirée in the first place."

Judith privately thought that it was no great wonder the youth had left the gathering. Indeed, she felt rather sorry for him—and for all his siblings. She had become acquainted with the public facts about the royal family as well as the private gossip, and she knew that the beautiful doors of their grand palaces concealed both secrecy and unhappiness.

The late Tsar Paul, who had died thirteen years ago, had nine children who had survived past childhood. Two of his daughters had died suddenly at the turn of the century, one in childbirth. Of the remaining seven, there were three sisters in the middle with two elder brothers and two younger brothers. The eldest, Emperor Alexander, was much respected and, at the age of thirty-seven, had already brought Russia through some very trying years. His brother,

Konstantin Pavlovich, was close in age at thirty-five and had great responsibilities of his own.

Maria Pavlovna, the nearest sister in age to those brothers, had accompanied her husband to the Congress of Vienna, where the Emperor Alexander was negotiating on Russia's behalf. That meant that the only sisters presently in St Petersburg were Catherine Pavlovna, already a widow at the age of twenty-six, and Anna Pavlovna, age nineteen. Unfortunately, neither was fond of the other, though Catherine and Alexander were said to be exceedingly close.

The two youngest brothers were Nikolai Pavlovich, age eighteen, and Mikhail Pavlovich, age sixteen. Judith had not heard a great deal of them apart from the fact that they both loved the Russian army and were happiest when they were out of the city.

Judith was sure that Mikhail Pavlovich had too many brothers to ever assume control of Russia, but he was the son of the emperor, which meant he was due great deference. And at his tender age, he must have felt awkward about that.

In Russia, though members of the royal family might be entertained by the first families in society, they were held up as the future rulers that they might become. If one might someday become an empress, one would be treated as such. To Judith, it all seemed rather exceedingly formal. Though she had never been in contact with the first members of England's royal family, she had been at events with minor royals in attendance. They received some deference, to be sure, but it was not so much greater than what was given to families like Louisa-Margaretta's, those with breeding and wealth.

"The poor young man," said Judith softly. "Mikhail

Pavlovich is so very young and, but for his own good fortune, might well have been killed."

She had heard all the same gossip as Louisa-Margaretta, and she knew that the ice in the center of the canal was customarily cleared of snow to permit people to pass through. The canals were like an icy road in wintertime, one where it was possible to drag along a sled full of goods or parcels without worrying about horses. The young prince was fortunate, for where he fell, some of the snow from the side of the canal had spilled into the very center. When added to the snow that had fallen earlier in the evening, it was just enough to cushion the young Mikhail Pavlovich's landing.

"It is unfortunate that nobody kept a closer eye on the boy." Mademoiselle Chatel sighed. "Indeed, people are saying that you meant to distract them, Miss Haddington."

"My dear!" Mrs Cluett exclaimed, her eyes darting nervously among the assembled parties.

"Don't take any notice of gossip like that," said Mr Cluett. "The less said, the better. Women have a way of twisting little things like this into the silliest stories." He seemed oblivious to the fact that he had just insulted everyone at the table.

Mademoiselle Chatel, who had a tendency to speak either not at all or far too much, continued her recounting. "You see, if the playing or singing had not been quite so fine, there is almost no chance that everyone at the party would have gathered at the back of the residence. Judith, I think you were one of the only people in the front room. Did you really observe nothing?"

Louisa-Margaretta, who had coloured in anger, whipped towards her friend. "Yes, Judith. Since I am apparently to blame for drawing the attention of the company away from young Mikhail Pavlovich, why did you not implore him to stay out of the cold?"

"I am hardly his keeper," said Judith, intending to defend herself. But what defense could she offer? She had hardly been an attentive companion to Miss Claudio.

"I am rather put out that you missed most of my singing," said Louisa-Margaretta. "Singing which had no murderous intent. I am hardly to blame if I am more skilled than most of the ladies in Petersburg put together. Indeed, perhaps Judith is to blame, as she plays for me when I sing in Derbyshire. There is little else to do there."

For a moment, Judith smiled. For while Derbyshire was a difficult place in certain ways, it was indeed a location where she and Louisa-Margaretta had spent many happy hours. Their time in the music room often began with Louisa-Margaretta crying, "I shall perish from boredom in this frozen place. Judith, write a tune and let me find words to sing, or Derbyshire will be the death of me." But by the end of it, both would be laughing and lighthearted. She could not think of their hours at the pianoforte with anything but the sweetest nostalgia.

Then, Judith realised that neither Mr nor Mrs Cluett seemed the slightest bit amused by their situation. And if she and Louisa-Margaretta lost the goodwill of their hosts, they might not have the resources they needed to hide the latter's delicate condition and resume their life in England with their reputations intact.

Accordingly, Judith cleared her throat. "It was so lovely to have music again," she said. "Perhaps the best way out is forward. Is there any chance of your family hosting a Christmas gathering, dear Mrs Cluett? That way, we could show the whole city how we celebrate in England, and it might be a cure for homesickness as well."

Mrs Cluett was shaking her head. "We do not have anyone who can cook English food. It would be nothing like a proper English Christmas."

"I'm sure I could instruct your cook in a dish or two," said Judith. She did not hide the fact that she had been brought up helping in the kitchen. To her parents, this had always been a point of pride, not one of shame, as it might have been for a grander family. "And it would be so very wonderful for all of the people who attended the last one."

Louisa-Margaretta had been sulking, but at a pointed look from Judith, she appeared to remember that she was supposed to be looking for a husband. Though Judith had been eager for Louisa-Margaretta to have her child in secret, without even considering an eleventh-hour marriage, Louisa-Margaretta herself took a different view of the matter. She had been hoping for some time to find a marriageable beau. "If some silly foreign fool will take me, I may as well marry," she had said to Judith. "And if I never return to England, that will be too soon for me. Let the masses say all they will about the date of my wedding. I shall never need to listen to them."

Judith had tried and failed to discover what Russian law had to say about the subject. If the child were born in England, the man legally wedded to the mother would be considered the child's father. Indeed, she had heard crude jokes all her life about large young women teetering to the church just days before the baby came. Those were the jokes that most angered Judith's parents, who refused to make sport of such ladies. Legally, though, at least the children were safe from illegitimacy, if not from gossip.

If Russian law said something different, it might be very unwise for Louisa-Margaretta to marry, but Judith had not yet ascertained a way of answering that particular question.

She would need to ask it in such a way that neither she nor her friend would ever be suspected of seeking out a quick marriage, and she had not quite worked out how to do so. Though her Russian had improved, her reading was very slow, and she was not sure which sort of legal volume might enlighten her. Certainly, nothing in the Cluetts' rather small collection of books, which were mostly in English and French.

Louisa-Margaretta, no doubt thinking of her husband-hunting tactics, joined in Judith's campaign to the Cluetts. Judith knew that Louisa-Margaretta must be thinking of using her singing voice to advantage in front of the many eligible young men who would be expected to attend.

"If you hold a ball," said Louisa-Margaretta, "and I sing something lovely, as I did at the last, nobody will ever speak of this again. Moreover, you shall be heroes."

"I'm sure we should not," said George Cluett, and it was the first sensible thing he had said all morning. "For holding a ball? Stuff and nonsense."

But Louisa-Margaretta continued. "The city would overflow with gratitude. Ladies would be falling over themselves to thank you, lending you their finery and their French cooks and all sorts."

Judith, exasperated, looked towards the ceiling. Her friend was certainly eager enough to charm her hosts with extravagant promises, and Judith had half a mind to try and stop her. But Louisa-Margaretta's words had already had their intended effect.

"Really, dearest," said Mrs Cluett. "We still feel very much like foreigners here, do we not? Perhaps we could establish ourselves before the emperor returns from Vienna. After all, they will soon finish their negotiations, and even if the roads are difficult, it will be only a matter of weeks before he returns." Mrs Cluett had acquired the habit shared by all the Russians of speaking of their leader in hushed, reverent tones. Though all seemed to respect the royal family, the sovereign was clearly considered quite special.

Thinking of the ruler, Judith felt a twinge of remorse and fear. Emperor Alexander I was in Vienna with a rather large party, speaking with other sovereigns about what ought to be done with France and the many borders that had been rearranged in recent years. Whenever Judith thought of all of the leaders, she wondered whether they had been in the room with the earnest but inexperienced Mr Morgan Ramsbury. Her dear fiancé had so much that he could have told these leaders, but Judith was not at all certain that he would be given a chance to speak. And if he were, would his audience know their own good fortune? Did they have any sense that they ought to listen to his advice?

When he'd seen that England was in danger of becoming so vehemently against Napoleon Bonaparte that they were willing to sacrifice all of the gains of the revolution, Morgan had felt compelled to join the negotiations as a minor assistant to a diplomat who was connected to his family. It was a very strange decision for a young man who had more than enough to live on, had never shown a great interest in making his way in the world, and had always preferred to devote his time and limited income to religious and charitable causes. Alarmed by the idea that the revolutionary ideals of France were to be entirely cut down by the other countries' desire for stability and revenge, he hoped to preserve some of the freedoms, perhaps even to expand on them. And he had agreed with Judith that her family required more time to accept their engagement. Though Judith was of age and could legally marry where she liked, it broke her heart to think of taking such a momentous step without the blessing of at least her father and her only sister. While Morgan was in France, she planned to wait in St Petersburg, thinking of all the ballads about waiting for a lover to return from the sea. Though in her case, of course, she was the one who would be doing most of the sailing, since Morgan had only the channel to cross. Oh, that the winds would be swift and bring him back to England! He was to come in spring at the latest, though very likely sooner, as there would be no reason to stay in Vienna after the conclusion of the negotiations. And after Judith returned with Louisa-Margaretta in summer, they were to be married.

Except she had not heard from Morgan, and the two letters she had received from her family indicated that he had not been in contact with them either. She could not shake the foreboding she felt that something had happened in France and was constantly trying to banish visions of beautiful and enticing Frenchwomen from her head. Surely, Morgan, who had traveled and met many women in his lifetime, would not have been susceptible. But if he were?

"Ladies all love a ball," said Mr Cluett. "Well then, we can give you ladies a ball. It might be the thing to wipe away some of these rather unpleasant inklings. Will that satisfy you?"

Louisa-Margaretta smiled, and Judith knew that the pleasure of getting her own way would keep her in spirits for some time.

"Yes," she said. "I should love to have a chance to entertain the company with English carols, and perhaps, if the furniture is suitably arranged, we may even have a little dancing."

Mademoiselle Chatel clapped her hands. "Oh, how

delightful! You must sing the Italian songs too. *Mamon* will love them."

"I can help with the arrangements," said Judith. "I know it is a great deal of work."

"It is not so difficult to set my voice to advantage," said Louisa-Margaretta with a degree of boasting that both annoyed and pleased Judith. "But yes, my dear friend, arrange away."

"I meant the arrangements for the ball," said Judith quietly. "But yes, Louisa-Margaretta, if you need something for the music, of course I can help."

Louisa-Margaretta looked rather like a cat. Judith knew that her friend was rather pleased with the impression that she had made and that even accusations of helping a murderer could not long temper her self-satisfaction.

"It will be worth it," said Mrs Cluett, blinking nervously. "Like you said, my dear, we mustn't have everyone reflecting on what happened to poor Mikhail Pavlovich and gossiping about any of you young ladies. These Russians can be rather hot-tempered, you know. Best we have them think on other things."

"Hot-tempered!" said Mademoiselle Chatel and babbled rapidly about some of the experiences she and her mother had gone through in southern Europe. She seemed to think that Venice, Sicily, Florence, and many other great cities had much more unreasonable populaces than St Petersburg. So Judith alone observed the meaningful looks exchanged between the Cluetts. Both of them had nerves that were hardly explained by a few whispers of gossip, and Judith wondered what they were hiding. Perhaps St Petersburg was not quite as safe as Madame Chatel had made it out to be.

4

———————

Louisa-Margaretta, as was her wont, disappeared promptly when there was work to be done. It was Judith who accompanied Mrs Cluett on calls to distribute invitations for the ball.

"We have to get the right sort of people to come, my dear," said Mrs Cluett. "You won't know such things, of course, being unmarried. Either the whole world will come, or they shall snub us and go to the theatre *en masse*. These Russians are rather difficult to manage, as I had mentioned."

"Yes, of course," said Judith. For a moment, she thought about telling Mrs Cluett that she had a great deal of experience herding groups of people about in her role as *de facto* rector's wife. Ever since Mama had died, Judith had been responsible for the many unpaid and onerous tasks that traditionally fell to the wives of clergymen, and she felt she had done them rather well. When Judith left home, Aunt Leah took on many of these duties, but in the absence of both Judith and Aunt Leah, they must be falling to Judith's only sister, Miriam. Imagine Miriam going on calls like a much older lady, talking over the finer points of the maintenance of the pews and the floral arrangements for Christ-mas! Judith had to suppress a laugh thinking of it, and she was overcome by a wave of homesickness as she did so. Ever since her family had moved to Derbyshire, things had never been right between her and Miriam. Either Judith was away, or Miriam was angry at Judith's having been away, or Miriam was pursuing an unsuitable young man.

Judith tried to stop herself from thinking of her sister. Louisa-Margaretta was the one who had pursued a truly undesirable man, and for this very reason, Judith needed all her wits about her now.

For just one moment, Judith allowed herself to imagine her own wedding, which would be small but rather perfect. Miriam was the most religiously open-minded family member she had, and while it probably would not be the case that Miriam herself would marry outside the faith, Judith thought her sister might not hold on to many objections about Morgan Ramsbury. Before she had left for Russia, she had not asked Miriam's opinion, and strangely enough, Miriam had not offered one. She had only blessed Judith's journey, asked careful questions about their manner of travel, and kissed her sister goodbye.

By the wedding, Judith decided, both Miriam and her father would be quite happy for her. There would be flow-ers, of course, and the scent of the few summer weeks during which Derbyshire was sweet and balmy. She hoped that they would be willing to attend, of course. Though the Marriage Act meant that Judith's marriage would be legal, if her father viewed it as illegitimate in God's eyes, she could hardly imagine him attending.

"I remember when I was unmarried still." Mrs Cluett was going on, quite oblivious to Judith's own worries. "Oh, how lovely, without so many responsibilities! I had my first child at nineteen, my last child at forty-three. You have no idea, of course, how much I miss them! And how much work it is to be a mother. We could not possibly have brought them here, of course."

Judith wondered why not but did not ask. The youngest child must be about twelve now. In fact, Judith would have understood many of Mrs Cluett's feelings, for she had helped raise her younger brothers and worried about them nearly as much as she worried about Miriam. She knew what it was to leave a beloved child behind in England.

"I am glad to be able to devote my hours to this event, Mrs Cluett," she said, hoping she was keeping her tone perfectly respectful. "As you noted, we spinsters have little else to occupy our time."

"That is all very well," said Mrs Cluett. "For we are going to have such a time convincing Cornelia van Beek to come. She is as a—Hello, dear Cornelia!"

An old, stout woman had opened the door to them. Mrs Cluett nearly shuddered, and Judith found herself surprised by the woman's stern expression.

Mrs Cluett cleared her throat. "This is our houseguest, Miss St Clair," she said. "Miss St Clair, my dear friend, Mrs Cornelia van Beek."

"I presume you have a first name, Miss St Clair," the lady said in a booming voice as she walked towards what appeared to be her parlour, clearly expecting the other two women to follow her. "I cannot abide this English love for last names. As if a young woman should have no first names, simply because she has only younger sisters!"

Judith, who privately agreed, spoke for the first time. "My Christian name is Judith, ma'am. I am very pleased to meet you."

She was not sure how to address the grand lady. Would

it be Mrs Beek, or Mrs van Beek? She suspected that the older lady's distaste for formality did not quite extend to wishing to be addressed as "Cornelia" by a much younger woman. Of all the people Judith had ever met, only the Quakers went in for such a radically egalitarian form of address, and even after a great deal of time in Quaker company, Judith had always felt uneasy with this custom.

"We have come to ask you to a party, as usual, dear Cordelia," twittered Mrs Cluett. "I know your hours are filled with many responsibilities, of course."

"Don't stand there like a fool," the lady said. "I will sit; you two can sit. There is tea and food on the sideboard. Help yourselves, and eat something. I cannot stand fine ladies with small appetites."

Judith reflected that the Dutch lady could hardly expect to enjoy the ball in that case. Most of the ladies they had met so far seemed to share the English preoccupation with taking small portions, though the incorrigible Louisa-Margaretta always took just as much food as she pleased. And when they were not in company, Madame Chatel ate exceedingly well. "I must eat to keep up my strength, or I cannot work," she had explained many times. "If I starve myself and cannot paint, I will starve for lack of money."

Seeing that the lady was sincere, Judith helped herself to a cup of what appeared to be coffee and two rather simple but hearty sandwiches. She was used to thin bread with very little inside, but these appeared to be packed with meat. Judith suspected that she would need the hot liquid to wash down the bites, and she added a large amount of milk to her coffee to disguise the taste of the rich fare.

"I understand your husband is from home, ma'am," Judith said. "How does he get on?"

For the first time, Cornelia van Beek smiled, and the

effect was extraordinary. Her face, which had been lined and severe, showed a sparkle and beauty that would otherwise have remained perfectly hidden.

"How does he get on, Judith? Well might you ask! He gets on terribly, and I told him that he would."

Judith found herself sinking into a chair so she could put down her refreshments on a small table before she started trembling. It was the first time she had heard anyone speak quite so frankly about the difficulties of the negotiations. There were rumbles amongst all the diplomats, of course, but they seemed to have too much reverence for Emperor Alexander to admit that his tactics might be failing.

"The Congress does not go well, then?" said Judith. "I had hoped that by this time, we might see considerable progress."

The older lady gave her a searching look. "Had you, then? I didn't take you for a fool. Every sovereign in Europe descending on the same city, each wanting a piece of Napoleon Bonaparte's loot, and none of them liking each other? Vienna, an excellent place for old enemies to meet new enemies. Ha!"

Judith's heart fluttered. "But surely, they will have to settle on something eventually? I am sure they would not all like to be in Vienna for many more weeks."

"I would like to be in Vienna," said Mrs van Beek with a rather garish grin. "It would be a sight easier at Christmas than this frozen purgatory, that much is certain. But my husband said I had to be here, old warhorse that I am, and I must say I agreed with him."

Mrs Cluett smiled. It was clear she could think of nothing to say. "Oh?"

Judith tried to continue. "Why did you need to stay,

ma'am? I am sure your presence would be helpful in Vienna."

Cordelia van Beek glared at her as if wondering whether she was being mocked. "I can play the diplomat's wife, though you might not believe it, young Judith. And I could have gone to Vienna with the men, not that they want women there, as they spend most of their time drinking and visiting actresses. I am here because our Russian friends are rather volatile, aren't they, Susannah? A nice system of government they've got here. A strong monarchy peppered with some very choice assassinations, that's what I always say to my husband. Never know when one would-be emperor will decide to bump someone off, so it's best to keep a watchman here. I'm sure you didn't come to learn more about the Russians, though I heard you saw Mikhail Pavlovich's little tumble onto the ice. What a farce that was! Must have been a weak person who couldn't harm a foolish and unattended boy, though I wish him no harm."

Mrs Cluett burst in, having finally gotten the opening in the conversation she had been unable to find. "No indeed. We came because we have an invitation for a ball to celebrate Christmas at our home. We should be honoured by your presence." She gave Judith a meaningful look.

"Oh please, won't you come?" Judith asked, though privately, she felt that it would be a very good thing if this forthright woman stayed away from their gathering. "It would be wonderful to speak with you again about the Congress."

The older lady peered at Judith. "Well, it gives me strength to see a young woman taking interest. All the other ladies only ask me if Bagration's wife is as beautiful as they say."

Judith looked down, but her hostess heard the question that had not been asked.

"Yes, even you wish to know, young Judith! Beautiful, yes, though I wouldn't be lining up to be with that merry widow. And if I were her, I wouldn't be bothered with any suitors either."

Judith swallowed, weighing the cost of one more question. She required more reports from the woman whose husband must, even now, be very close to Morgan, but she was afraid that the "old warhorse" might guess her true motive.

"Ah, I might come, now," Mrs van Beek said, and her tone had softened so that it was almost affectionate. "If only because I've heard that your Louisa-Margaretta is teaching our Ivo Solier some manners. Ha! If that man has musical genius *and* respectability, he will be truly great."

Judith could not feel relief that they had accomplished their aim, though in the carriage, Mrs Cluett praised her and laughed with relief at being free of her "friend" Cordelia. She could only think of Morgan, sitting in Vienna, locked in a situation that seemed to combine hopeless negotiation with unspeakable debauchery.

By the time they arrived home to find Louisa-Margaretta staring listlessly out the window, a novel closed in her lap, Judith was cross.

"Thank you for your help," she hissed as soon as Mrs Cluett left the room. "Were you planning to assist us at any point, Louisa-Margaretta, since you claimed to long for a ball?"

5

———

Louisa-Margaretta had been feeling ready for sleep since the moment of her waking. But on hearing Judith's insult, she sprang to life.

"I do not long for a ball," she said. "As you well know, my reputation depends on this ball. Perhaps even my life, for I'm sure a wealthy husband would provide for an accoucheur. If I am left in the hands of a country hag, paid handsomely for her discretion, I may very well die in childbirth."

Judith did not sigh at these dramatics. Her poise, as always, was irritating. In Louisa-Margaretta's company, she had shown every inch of her principled upbringing for the past several months. And Louisa-Margaretta fancied that she could read her friend's thoughts.

"Think of the poor wee child," Judith must be thinking. "Louisa-Margaretta may be talking a good deal of nonsense, but it would be unpardonable to call this child's mother a weak and horrid fool, though that is plainly what she is."

Louisa-Margaretta bristled at this imagined dialogue. "Never you mind, Judith," she said sharply. "I am more than capable of finding my own husband. In fact, I do not know why I should have thought you would be any help in this matter. Finding a proper husband is not an area in which I would expect you to have any expertise."

At last, Judith's eyes widened, and Louisa-Margaretta took a grim satisfaction in seeing the expression on her friend's face. It resembled the way she'd felt as a child every time she turned out one of her governesses. Each young woman would come, lured by Mama's indefatigable promises and the unusually high wages. The good Mrs Haddington was so kind, so energetic, that by the time any young woman had spent half an hour with her, she would be convinced that one daughter could not possibly cause too much trouble.

But Louisa-Margaretta had always had a rather peculiar knack for causing as much trouble as possible.

"Morgan is your cousin," said Judith. It was a rather simple fact, yet her voice rang with unspoken reproaches.

"Am I his keeper?" asked Louisa-Margaretta. "I'll answer that. No, I am not. And it is exceedingly silly for you to go on about Vienna. My cousin is well provided for there, and I have no doubt he spends his days running great stacks of parchment from one pretty little house to another." She was still in the mood to provoke her friend, but she noticed that Judith had let a little smile escape.

"It is reasonable," Judith said quietly. "He has taken on this risk to his own person, all due to his political beliefs. I would be silly not to worry."

Louisa-Margaretta shook her head so vigorously that her carefully pinned tresses were at great risk of coming loose. "What, you expect dear Cousin Morgan to throw it all up and travel to Elba? Or, madder still, to come into some fortune we've never heard of and set up a Viennese harem?"

"You have said quite enough," said Judith. She left the room, her head bowed.

Louisa-Margaretta's face fell into a pout. She clenched her fists, blinking back the dampness that seemed to have overtaken her eyes. One hand strayed to her stomach, not as large as it would become later, but she pushed away the impulse to touch it. Judith was being impossible, and the whispers of conscience that floated by her mind like so many snowflakes were blown away.

Now, she had a mission.

"Dear Susannah," she said, sweeping into the room where Mrs Cluett stood in hushed conference with her housekeeper. "Did you not say that you were greatly looking forward to the concert that is to be held in the palace tomorrow?"

"I am not quite sure about that, dear," murmured the lady. She spoke softly, as if she expected spies around every corner.

"Well," said Louisa-Margaretta. "I require an invitation. And I need to speak to that composer again—Ivo Polier? Or whatever his name was. I'm sure he will wish me to sing."

"We have a great deal to do for the ball," said Mrs Cluett. It seemed as close to a protest as she was willing to offer.

"Not to worry. I do intend to charm all the royals, you know. Only you have simply got to secure me an invitation. And send your maid to alter one of my dresses. And do lend me some of your jewelry. It won't do if I go as a pauper."

"Only that?" said Mrs Cluett, and if there was a wry note in her voice, Louisa-Margaretta chose not to hear it.

"Only that, yes," said Louisa-Margaretta, leaving the room before Mrs Cluett could say anything against her.

6

The Kazan Cathedral was the grandest religious building that Judith had ever seen. Though she had visited a great deal of different cathedrals in the course of her upbringing, she had never before felt the presence of God as strongly as she did in the Kazanski Sabor, as the locals called it. Judith had been pronouncing the word for church "soh-bor," as this fit better with the way it was spelled in the Cyrillic alphabet, but Mrs Cluett's maid swiftly corrected her. Apparently, all of the Russian words had a sort of "ah" sound on unaccented syllables if Judith had understood Masha correctly. This explained some of Judith's difficulties conversing with the local population, as she was relying primarily on words she had memorised from an old Russian grammar. It would take her some time to say "kho-lad-na" for cold instead of "kho-lod-no," but at least her complaints might be soon understood.

She practiced the new word as she entered the Kazanski Sabor. "Kho-lod-no," whispered Judith, so softly she would not be heard. The cathedral was cold, but it was warmer than the bitter streets. On entering, Judith found that she was able to take off the fur hat that Mrs Cluett had loaned her.

As Judith stood in the back of the cathedral, uncertain whether she would be welcome, an old woman gestured towards her, frowning. Judith finally managed to say in Russian that she did not understand, upon which the woman's expression softened. The woman touched the thick, woolen shawl that was covering her hair then gestured towards Judith.

"Oh!" said Judith, finally understanding. She took up her own scarf, pulling it over her hair. One look around the place showed her that all of the women were covering their heads. Though Judith had learned in the course of her education that Muslim and Jewish women often covered their hair, she had not known that the same was true for Orthodox Russians. Indeed, Judith's education had rather neglected Russia, a country that was seldom mentioned with a language that was considered impossible and impractical. Judith was determined not to be like the Cluetts, cloistered away in a francophone community that knew and cared very little for the troubles of the common people. If she had to stay in this land for a year or more, she would learn as much of the language and customs as she could.

Though even this was not her main duty in coming to the cathedral. She hoped to light a candle for Morgan. God would understand, she knew, if she did not follow the Anglican steps to the letter. She had long before ceased believing that God was selective when it came to the manner of worship.

Judith loved the smell of the place. There was something about the scent, fresh bread and soft incense, that made her wish to sit. But everyone else was standing. She did not even see the weak and infirm go to the wall, as they might have in England. With her rudimentary Russian, Judith understood almost nothing of what the priest was saying in Old Church Slavonic, but she lost herself in quiet reflection all the same.

By the time she left, she was so absorbed in her own thoughts that she nearly missed a strange sight. A carriage was passing by, and in the very small window, she was able to see Anna Pavlovna, looking considerably more stormy than she had the other night. All around her, carriages stopped, and the people inside them piled out. Judith remembered one of the ladies from the gathering at the Prussian ambassador's home, and in spite of the cold, she approached her.

"Why has everyone left their carriages?"

"Why don't you have a carriage yourself, if I may beg your pardon?"

Judith shook her head. "The Cluetts live far too near. It was easier for me to walk."

The woman gave a throaty laugh. "There is no sense in walking in this city. Though when one of the royal family passes, we all must be outside like serfs. It is the greatest indignity, though I suppose I ought to be thankful that they travel quickly. I try to go out when I know that they will not be visiting, but there are so very many of them!"

The royal carriage had passed, and people were climbing back into their carriages all around Judith.

"Truly, we can take you back."

Judith realized her teeth were already chattering from the cold. She ought to have started walking. Instead, standing outside and gawking had left her frozen.

"I will walk, thank you," she said. But as she went back to the Cluetts', she remained uneasy. How strange that everyone had to stand in the snow when someone from the royal family happened to be passing! It made her wonder about the attack on Mikhail Pavlovich. Perhaps there was more resentment against him and his siblings than she had been able to discern.

Judith decided to keep an even closer watch on the way that the first families of St Petersburg responded to royalty. An attempted murder would be a strange way to demonstrate resentment at small inconveniences, but after what the whole world had seen in France, Judith was well aware that long injustices could easily transform into larger troubles.

7

L ouisa-Margaretta thought she had met most of the nobility of St Petersburg. Her impression from the party at the Prussian Ambassador's residence was that there were not many in the first circles and that at any given event, one might rub elbows with various members of the royal family.

The concert soon proved that she had been quite mistaken.

As it turned out, when one was invited to the Winter Palace for a formal concert, there was no question of not attending. All of the noble families in the city, even those full of recluses and paupers, felt obligated to turn out for the evening's entertainment. Louisa-Margaretta recognised a few faces from the party at the Prussian ambassador's house, but many of the elegant ladies and gentlemen appeared to be new. And there were so many of them that it was hard to get anywhere near the stage during the interval.

All of this would not have necessarily disturbed Louisa-Margaretta had it not been for the performance itself. The soprano who was singing some of Ivo Solier's work was impeccable. True, she was older even than Louisa-Margaretta, but it was clear she was still a great beauty. And the ease with which she trilled her way through even the strangest melodies was disturbing. Louisa-Margaretta wondered why she had been convinced that Mr Solier would regard her as some sort of muse, perhaps even to the point of wishing to marry her. A well-born English girl, whose practice had never been as frequent or as disciplined as her mother had wished it to be, would never be able to compete with an accomplished musician.

There was no time to spare for regrets, yet Louisa-Margaretta wondered whether Judith had not been correct in her assertions that they ought to study at some sort of profession. For now, it was too late for Louisa-Margaretta to apply herself to an art like music. She would never be hired as a performer, though she was safe in St Petersburg, and word of her working for wages would never get back to Mama. If shame was no longer a barrier, her lack of skill was. She ought to have spent every spare hour practising, then she would not need to weave through the crowd, looking for a husband and bestowing a simpering smile on every red-faced gentleman who passed.

In the first interval, Louisa-Margaretta tried to meet the city's eligible nobles while standing next to Mrs Cluett. They were joined by one of Mrs Cluett's friends, who had a pale brow and a diffident air. Louisa-Margaretta hadn't bothered learning the lady's name. But after several minutes of idle chatter about the lovely instruments, Louisa-Margaretta found herself growing impatient. If she were going to succeed in the society of this strange city, she would have to learn more names. And she would have to force her acquaintances to introduce her to those of greater consequence. Only this way could she find herself a prospect.

"I see that the young Anna Pavlovna is in attendance," she said to the lady, smiling. "I had little opportunity to speak to her the other evening. What an accomplished young lady!"

In fact, Louisa-Margaretta had heard rumors that Anna Pavlovna was not an easy young lady at all. This little royal had almost no power, but she behaved as if she were an empress like her late grandmother. She was rumoured to lock herself in her room for days on end in protest of any edict that she did not wish to follow.

It was almost enough to make Louisa-Margaretta like her.

But the lady, who from her accent appeared to be Spanish, only sniffed. "Anna Pavlovna will not speak to us," she said. "She seems to like those strange mystics well enough, and she will pass the afternoon with her brothers. But her sisters? Ordinary ladies? She has little time for the likes of us."

Louisa-Margaretta's spirits fell, but she kept up a brave smile. "Indeed, as a lone sister with many brothers, I know what it is to be always hunting and thinking of sport."

This garnered gasps from both ladies.

"Indeed, no," said Mrs Cluett. "It is uncommon for a young woman to hunt, even in England," she said to the other lady. "Here, it would be unthinkable for the young Anna Pavlovna."

Louisa-Margaretta persisted. "But do not noble ladies hunt? I am sure I heard someone at the soiree the other night speaking of such a thing."

In fact, one of the ladies had been talking a great deal about hunting. But Louisa-Margaretta, who had been determined to avoid the conversation, could recall little of what had been said.

"It was that woman in the black gown. I believe her patronymic was Maximovna?"

The two ladies exchanged glances.

"Vladilena Maximovna takes delight in sharing the most shocking things," grumbled the Spanish lady. "I pray you would not turn to that lady for your lessons about Russian society."

"Why not turn to me?" came a voice over her shoulder. "Or is it to be presumed that, because I have a profession, I am no longer an authority on my own motherland?"

The Spanish lady and Mrs Cluett had the good grace to blush, but Louisa-Margaretta only looked more closely. The lady who had spoken of hunting was wearing her black gown again. Though the garment was well made, the fabric did not look well suited for a palace at all. In fact, the lack of decolletage made the Maximovna woman look much warmer than any other woman in the room, a state Louisa-Margaretta envied.

"What is your profession, then?" she asked. "I have heard you speak only of hunting."

"I am a physician" was the crisp answer. "But I tend to be the doctor of last resort for most families. They come to me because they have no money or because all my male colleagues have failed them."

Louisa-Margaretta was intrigued. "And do you also fail them at times?"

"Generally not. But medicine cannot cure all evils. I know when I am beaten."

"How interesting," said Louisa-Margaretta. "Perhaps you would like to meet my friend."

The lady did not immediately acquiesce. "An ill friend? I

shall have to advise you, I have little by way of medicine with me."

"No, a friend with a profession," said Louisa-Margaretta.

"A rare bird in this city, then," said Vladilena Maximovna. "I shall grant you, nobody has trouble with exploiting the toiling peasant women. But the same men who would not think of freeing their serfs will insist that a noblewoman is not fit to be a doctor."

"Indeed," said Louisa-Margaretta soothingly. For the first time, she wished that she had come to the concert in Judith's company. The rector's daughter, in spite of her impeccable manners, was much more interested in the place of women in society. While Louisa-Margaretta would have been content to be rich and independent, Judith was interested in the work of Mary Wollstonecraft. She took the entire subject of "women's rights" so seriously that Louisa-Margaretta was forever telling her to stop speaking about it. The whole thing was so terrifically boring compared to a good hunt.

Louisa-Margaretta looked at the darkly clad lady, hoping at some point she might be able to wangle an invitation to a Russian hunt. But first, she would need to ingratiate herself with the right set so as to hunt for a husband.

"Madame Chatel, this is my new friend. My good friend, please meet this intelligent and accomplished painter. Surely, the royal family would love to avail themselves of her services! She is unparalleled, and I always think that for a young woman such as Anna Pavlovna, a female portraitist is by far the safest choice."

"I would not presume to be the finest portraitist for anyone," said Madame Chatel firmly. "My dear Miss Haddington, you misrepresent me to this good lady. If you'll pardon me, madam, your name?"

The doctor only laughed. "Vladilena Maximovna," she

said shortly. Though she had spoken English with Louisa-Margaretta, her French was also excellent. "I daresay there will be little interest. The palace only starts paying for portraits of ladies when they have borne at least ten children."

Her voice carried so much bitterness that Louisa-Margaretta was not sure how to respond. "Perhaps we might interest you yourself in a portrait, then?" she asked.

"Really," said Madame Chatel, insistent, but the doctor only shook her head.

"I am not offended, but I am in possession of a looking glass. Nobody needs to know what I look like. Madame Chatel, if you can force my children to sit still for you, we will speak of some very handsome commissions."

The Frenchwoman's smile was icy. "Of course, how lovely. Louisa-Margaretta, we should take our seats."

At home in England, they all would have been seated for the concert after the person of highest rank arrived. But it appeared that at this palace, things were to proceed very differently. Though the best seats were reserved for members of the royal family, people seemed to come and go at will, almost as if they were at the opera. It was not orderly, as it would have been in England, and Louisa-Margaretta was surprised to feel a pang of homesickness. Ever since she had come to Russia, she had been surprised to feel a weakness in herself which she thought ought to have been confined to other people. It was as if her name, money, and family reputation had provided an invisible buttressing she had never known she required. Now that she was alone and soon to be judged on the basis of one weak and wanton moment, she missed the deference that she had thought she would always be able to claim.

"What on earth were you thinking," snapped Madame

Chatel as soon as they were out of the doctor's hearing. "You can never speak of the nobility with such rudeness."

"I was hardly rude," said Louisa-Margaretta, surprised. "You have painted such portraits before, and I am sure they would not be displeased with your work!"

"Of course they would not," said Madame Chatel. "My work is excellent."

But that was not the end of the matter. The French-woman's eyes narrowed as she looked at the royal family, now assembled near the stage, and turned back to Louisa-Margaretta. "It is impertinent to suggest anything to them," she whispered hastily. "If we are seen as making demands on such personages, we will be turned out of polite society entirely."

Louisa-Margaretta laughed. "What, simply for making an innocent offer?"

"Yes! My child, you have no idea of what you speak. You know nothing of the danger. So if you wish to stay in this place, for the first time in your life, hold your tongue."

The ballroom was now filled with people. It would have been the height of rudeness to leave just when the violinists were setting their bows with purpose on their legs, when the offensive soprano was striding back to the front to entertain with her glorious voice.

Louisa-Margaretta left anyway, which was foolish. But even she could not stomach the cold outdoors. She wouldn't mind her feet getting cold during the walk home, but she would have to draw the line at losing a toe or two. Or perhaps even losing a limb. The night was very cold indeed. Also, as she had learned from poor Mikhail Pavlovich, it was not safe to stride along the canals in the dark night, not even in the finest part of the city.

So she left the room and retreated to the powder room

that had been discreetly provided for the ladies. Louisa-Margaretta paced, simmering with her protector's accusations, around the part of the room that had a large mirror. Though there was no fire, there were chairs, and one of them was occupied by an old woman who was snoring.

Relegated to a windowless room with an ancient lady, Louisa-Margaretta felt the unfamiliar sensation of defeat creeping back into her. Before she had been foolish enough to have a liaison with a married man, she had never felt as hopeless as she did now. It would have been silly for her to lose her heart, but she could not even claim to have done that. No, her time with Mr Chandler was not filled with love, and still, she was paying just as high a price as any idiot girl whose head had been turned by nosegays and poetry.

And she was not alone.

Next to her, in the mirror, the pale visage of a woman in black looked at Louisa-Margaretta with pity. "You didn't like hearing someone else sing it, then?"

Louisa-Margaretta blinked. "No, I don't care."

This got a chuckle from the doctor. "Of course you don't. I'm sure it comes as a shock when so recently, everyone was listening to your voice. If it's any consolation, I liked it better when you sang it."

Louisa-Margaretta's feelings of self-pity dissolved as she turned to face the woman. "You don't need to condescend to me."

"I'm not. That Muscovite soprano would have a lovely voice were she not the most vapid, unkind human I have ever spoken with. At least you seem to have a little more wit about you."

Louisa-Margaretta glared. "I don't know why you feel called to insult me, Miss—Mrs—" she could remember nothing of the woman's name. "Whoever you are, Doctor."

"Vladilena Maximovna," snapped the woman. "It is not a difficult name if you would make the effort."

"Could I not just refer to you as Madame Doctor or something like that? You are the only woman I know who is also a doctor, though one of my cousins is a physician and always tells us to carry strange weights and metal plates about our person. Apparently, it is very beneficial to the digestion, or so he tells me."

Her face took on a strange colour. "You would call me Madame Doctor? Yes, that would do very well. I would certainly not be offended, though you would be one of the first to address me that way. Most do not wish to acknowledge my education."

Louisa-Margaretta nodded. "I shall. Madame Doctor, tell me when the next interval is. I'm not going to have any success at this concert, but I cannot hide any longer in this horrid little room."

The woman gave half a smile. "I always like to see some fighting spirit. We may go together, then. You must tell me more about your cousin's work with the weights."

Louisa-Margaretta shook her head. "I never listen to him when he speaks of it. And I refuse to wear the weights; it is a silly idea. My digestion has always been strong."

The woman with the long name shook her head. "I think there might be something in it, although I would require proof."

They left together. The empty hall now seemed even colder, and Louisa-Margaretta found herself wishing she had dressed as practically as the doctor. Outside the ballroom, they could hear applause then the muted roar of conversation.

"Come, it will be ending now," said the Russian woman, sighing. "You can stop hiding here. One cannot run from these ghastly affairs, but at least they are never long."

As they made for the ballroom, they were ambushed by another woman. She was not Russian, Louisa-Margaretta was sure. Something about her spoke of more time spent in the sun. Though everyone had told Louisa-Margaretta about the long summer days of St Petersburg, she could hardly believe they would ever come. Most of the Russians she met seemed to be wilting from lack of sunshine.

"Not enjoying the concert, then, ladies?" said the woman, a look of sympathy on her face. Louisa-Margaretta thought there was a bit of smugness in her expression, but it was not unkind. She had a small figure and was almost as thin as Judith, but for all that, there was a great deal of beauty in her face. Next to this young woman and the doctor, Louisa-Margaretta felt exceptionally tall.

"I came because my brother asked me," said the doctor. "And because even I can't refuse every invitation from this quarter. One can only be indisposed so many times for *such* hosts. I can't say I found it interesting."

"And you, my friend?" said the woman, pressing Louisa-Margaretta's hand with a warmth that marked her out as someone from the south of Europe. "What did the music make you feel?"

Louisa-Margaretta pulled her hand away. "Very little. I find this sort of thing very frivolous, if you must know."

She had intended to be provocative, as she had given up her aim for the evening and wished only for the comfort of a return to the Cluetts' home. But to her surprise, the woman laughed.

"Indeed, that makes a great deal of sense! Though we often look to music as a conduit of spiritual truth, it means but little when compared to the manifold opportunities we have for prayer and genuine reflection."

Louisa-Margaretta's first instinct was to look around for Judith. These mad religious types were always best passed along to the rector's daughter. Though Louisa-Margaretta had been forced into prayer and dull "reflection" many times by her own mother, she found the Anglican God a rather disapproving old man and preferred to avoid speaking of him. With the Quakers, she always felt marginally more tolerant, if only because they prized silence and therefore didn't go on about things. In their vast silences, Louisa-Margaretta reflected on many things and found that her thoughts turned very occasionally to the divine. That is, provided she was well fed, for when she had taken an insufficient breakfast, there was nothing that could keep her thoughts from bread and meat.

This young woman, it appeared, was not one for a vow of silence. She had continued talking, this time about saints and pilgrimages. Louisa-Margaretta could see the doctor looking both irritated and wary, her expression frozen in barely veiled distaste.

"But you must come to one of our meetings," the dark woman was saying, her eyes bright and her voice even more musical with its strange singsong accent. "Then, we can discuss these matters properly, away from the florid vapidity of these society affairs."

Louisa-Margaretta was about to shake her head, but then she reflected that she could offer no reason to stay away. The only task before her was accompanying Mrs Cluett on calls to invite important personages to attend their sad party. Perhaps it would do her good to listen to a group of women nattering on about God. It would lend a bit of variety to days spent under the weight of Susannah Cluett's judgements, and it would be some escape from looking for a husband. For the only thing worse than fending off legions of dull suitors during a London season appeared to be sitting about in St Petersburg, ignored by all the men. For one sick moment, Louisa-Margaretta wondered if others knew the reason that she was so urgently seeking a husband. Then, she recalled that Judith, Madame Chatel, and Mademoiselle Chatel, while all maddening in their own ways, would hardly have decided to shelter her in such a cold and inconvenient city while making her secret public. No, it must be that none of the Russian men were interested in marrying her, which was somehow worse.

And, indeed, the women had hardly been friendly. The zealot who stood before her, beaming and waiting, was the first person to trouble herself over Louisa-Margaretta's comfort.

"I would be honoured," said Louisa-Margaretta firmly. "Only let me know the time and place."

The woman beamed as if she could not possibly have expected an affirmative answer from such a distinguished guest. "How lovely! There will be a few of us tomorrow, about three, if the weather holds. I am staying with my dear friend Daria Ippolitovna and her family. And Vladilena Maximovna, I very much hope we can finally expect you to join us."

"I will come once," said the doctor, narrowing her eyes. "Then, you may stop accosting me at every gathering. And you will leave Miss Louisa-Margaretta Haddington alone after that, will you not?"

Louisa-Margaretta was impressed by how well this relative stranger pronounced her name, and her new friend's recitation was equally accurate.

"Miss Louisa-Margaretta Haddington," said the young

woman. "You may call me Mary Josefa. It is not the name I was given but the one I was called to take. One day, at the end of a long pilgrimage to the shrine of Our Lady of Sorrows, I happened upon a statue."

"And your surname?" said Louisa-Margaretta.

"Claudio," the young woman said. "I believe you may be acquainted with my cousin?"

"Louisa-Margaretta," said Madame Chatel, bustling over to their little grouping with a studied expression of kind exasperation. "We have been looking all over for you. Our carriage is waiting. Ladies," she said, with the narrowest of smiles.

They were hardly out of hearing of that party when the Frenchwoman started in with her reproofs. "How could you think to make those sort of promises? You hardly know that Russian woman, and she has a most unsavory reputation. Did you hear nothing of what I said to you?"

Louisa-Margaretta thought of the doctor in her plain, modest clothing. She could have passed for a stern Quaker lady, and perhaps she would have been one had she lived in England.

"The doctor hardly seemed 'unsavory' to me. And someone told me she was rich."

Madame Chatel had taken Louisa-Margaretta's cloak, and she thrust it at her. "Oh, she is rich enough, to be sure. But she flouts the rules of society. And if anyone knows the danger of this, I do. She is not the sort of person with whom we ought to be associating."

"Oh, come now, madame," said Louisa-Margaretta, her pride still smarting from the way she had been ignored by most of the concertgoers. "Would it not be exceedingly vain to think that anyone observes what we do or cares how we conduct ourselves?"

"We are always observed," Madame Chatel said sharply. "And if you'd ever seen a friend sent to the guillotine, you would think carefully about how you conduct yourself. I had little interest in this concert, but I came. Even less in a ball at the Cluetts', but I am running about speaking of it as if I hadn't a care in the world apart from dancing."

Louisa-Margaretta frowned. She had always believed that Madame Chatel loved dancing and dining with her well-heeled patrons and had never supposed that she did so out of fear. "Why do you not concentrate on your painting if that is what you wish? Surely, it is understandable that you wish to earn."

Louisa-Margaretta said this like one who had not been born to great riches, and she was rather proud of how sincere and reasonable she sounded. Though she realised that she had most often heard such sentiments from her father, who had worked for his fortune, rather than from people of her mother's social standing. Louisa-Margaretta had once found working for one's living rather common, though the experience of earning her own paltry salary had made her think on the matter somewhat differently. And now that she was to be a mother, she wished that she had taken Judith up on her idea of writing and selling music together. Maybe then, she wouldn't be in such a strange, frigid city. This place made the cold winters of Derbyshire seem warm and cozy.

Madame Chatel was glaring at Louisa-Margaretta. Her voice was low, though there was so much commotion in the room that Louisa-Margaretta was sure nobody would have heard even a shouted conversation. "I cannot earn nearly as well if I present myself as only a pauper with a set of paints! I must indicate that one of my greatest concerns is to mingle in society. That is, I must pretend that this is so. Otherwise, I shall never get the sort of commissions I deserve. If anyone suspects my motives are mercenary, if I give the barest hint of boredom at a silly concert like this one, the rubles shall evaporate."

Louisa-Margaretta took her cloak from Madame Chatel, fastening it about herself quickly. "To the carriage, then. So you do not actually enjoy any of this?"

Madame Chatel gave an exasperated sigh, reminding Louisa-Margaretta very strongly of her mama. "I am an artist, Louisa-Margaretta. I enjoy my daughter's company and that of a few friends, and beyond that, I would much rather paint. Unlike your Ivo Solier, I am not one for parties."

They stepped outside, and the air was even colder than it had been, though for once, there was no wind. Louisa-Margaretta was glad that it was not snowing, though her skin felt tender and prickly in the cold. At least the Cluetts' carriage, if not exactly warm, would keep them safe.

She could not stop a small burst of pleasure at hearing the composer described as "her" Ivo Solier, though she knew it was not very apt. He had not shown any interest in her during this concert, certainly, and she was now aware that her voice was nothing very special for him either. But the idea of being anyone's wife allayed some of her pressing anxiety for her future child, and being the wife of a musical genius would certainly have some cachet.

"Well, you can rely on me not to reveal your disdain for this sort of thing," said Louisa-Margaretta. They had almost reached the carriage, and she believed that she would have the last word. Nobody liked to stay outside in such weather and argue.

Nobody, that is, but Madame Chatel.

"You will do better," said Madame Chatel. "You will stop

using my name and my reputation to try and get attention from these Russian nobles. And you will stop having anything to do with that despicable Vladilena Maximovna."

Louisa-Margaretta, for the first time, was genuinely interested in saying the name of the woman. "Vladi, hmm. Vladilena Maximova. If she is invited to the palace, she can hardly be so out of favor."

Madame Chatel sniffed. Though they had been speaking English, something about her sniff sounded distinctly French. "Her brother is more suave than she, and for the sake of who her family is, even the inhabitants of palaces cannot fully shun her. But she is not the sort of friend you should make, and now that you are aware of that fact, I consider the matter settled."

So it was Madame Chatel, then, who got to have the last word. She swept into the carriage before Louisa-Margaretta, and they could hardly speak of such things openly before Mrs Cluett.

"Did you enjoy the concert, then?" Mrs Cluett asked Louisa-Margaretta. Her body was entirely hidden by a large and heavy traveling rug. "I fear you rather missed the most impressive number."

"Yes, it was very nice," said Louisa-Margaretta, setting her feet on one of the hot bricks at the bottom of the carriage. She tried to glare at Madame Chatel, but that lady was already otherwise engaged. The Russian carriages usually had little by way of windows, since all inhabitants had to be kept warm enough to stay alive. Their tiny window showed a view of the icy Neva before the coachman turned along one of the canals.

With the conversation finished, Louisa-Margaretta's thoughts turned to her friend Judith. How Judith would have loved both the strange doctor and the dark mystic, with all of her warm invitations! Louisa-Margaretta liked practical arguments, not philosophical ones, but Judith would happily have spoken to both of them about professions and prophets. Louisa-Margaretta's lips curled into a smile when she thought of how she could tease her friend while describing the evening.

Her smile fell away when she remembered that she and Judith were not speaking.

8

I n the cold afternoon, Judith considered making another trip to the Kazan Cathedral. She was the only person who had not secured an invitation for the concert the evening before, apart from Mademoiselle Marie Chatel, who was even less practiced at ingratiating herself into such social circles. So it happened that the two of them were together in the morning. They were alone in Mrs Cluett's sitting room, as all of the other ladies had risen late and then excused themselves. All but Louisa-Margaretta, who seemed not to have risen at all. Against her better judgment, Judith felt a pang of sympathy. She had always heard from ladies that mornings were a particularly torturous time when they were in a delicate condition, and Louisa-Margaretta still had to go to considerable pains to hide the truth.

"Marie," said Judith, "I was wondering if you might help me plan some games for our little gathering. Do you think that the Russians would like to play our traditional games, or would they rather dance?"

Judith had been feeling uneasy about the party, and it

had not escaped her notice that Mrs Cluett seemed more anxious than excited. Though Judith hated to admit the thought, even to herself, something about inviting all the same people who had been present when Mikhail Pavlovich was pushed off the bridge felt rather dangerous. It was as if they were also inviting another such calamity. But surely, at a little Christmas party, nobody would dare to try such a thing a second time? She wished she could ask Louisa-Margaretta, but they were not speaking. And no one else amongst the ladies had a nose for murder.

Marie sighed. "I haven't the slightest idea. Judith, I must tell you, when Mama said we were coming to Russia, I thought of running away. I never wanted to come here at all. Now that we have arrived, it seems there is always some sort of trouble."

Judith smiled. "It is not quite as bad as all that, surely? This is a beautiful city, and Russian is a lovely language. I never would have learned anything of it had I not come here. It is not considered the right sort of language for an English lady."

"That is why I despise it," said the younger woman, walking over to a windowsill but recoiling at the draught that she encountered there. "All those strange, guttural sounds, and the alphabet is nonsense! I was always hopeless at Greek too."

"Where would you have liked to spend Christmas?" said Judith, taking out her work bag. They always seemed to need warmer garments, so she was trying to use the last of her wool to make a shawl that would help during the cold and dark hours.

"I don't know," grumbled Mademoiselle Marie. "A thousand miles south of here."

"But where, exactly?" said Judith, coaxing. It was a

method she had learned as the eldest of all her sisters and brothers. Every time one of her siblings complained, Judith forced them to imagine the object of their desires with perfect specificity. Even when the treat they wished for could not be delivered, which was rather more likely than not given the fortunes of the St Clair family, the imagining served to lighten the mood.

"We could go back to Italy," said Marie. "But I don't care where we live, particularly. I just wish my mother would settle on one place. You and Louisa-Margaretta are the only real friends I've had in ages."

This was a rather sorry declaration.

Louisa-Margaretta swept into the room in that moment, and she seemed quite keen on ignoring them. She did not even look at Marie Chatel.

A dear friend, indeed.

"I am going out," Louisa-Margaretta said. "I couldn't find anyone else, but you may tell them all that I am at Daria Ippolitovna's home. I gather it is a respectable one."

"You have been invited to one of Mary Josefa's prayer meetings," said Judith, impressed in spite of herself. "I hear those are the talk of Petersburg. But would Mrs Cluett approve of your going?"

There was a flash of triumph in Louisa-Margaretta's eyes, quickly suppressed. She would want to pretend not to be overly pleased with the accomplishment. "It doesn't do to sit idly by," said Louisa-Margaretta. "The Lord helps those who help themselves, Judith."

She did not bother pretending that she needed to answer Judith's question. It was as if Judith had never asked it. Louisa-Margaretta simply left, her head held high as she walked the few steps to the warm carriage that awaited her.

Judith watched Louisa-Margaretta's departure, her face

twisted with annoyance. They had rowed before, of course, but never in such close quarters. The ambassador's house had large enough rooms for entertaining, but bedrooms were scarce. Louisa-Margaretta and Judith had to sleep in the same room, and so the night before, Judith had slipped in and out of dreams as she waited for her friend to return. Her mind would not let her rest until Louisa-Margaretta was in the other bed, breathing softly.

"Do you think I could be invited to such a prayer meeting?" said Marie. "I suppose they are very choosey about their invitations, but if I asked Louisa-Margaretta, do you think she might take me?"

Judith could not say definitively. Louisa-Margaretta, when she was not in a humour to speak with even Judith, could be unconscionably rude.

"We can pray here," Judith said with quiet conviction. One of the gifts she had learned at her father's knee was the ability to pray with anyone, in any place. It settled her heart during the most trying times, and as she said the familiar words, she could feel the turmoil in her heart starting to lift.

Though her words were sincere, they were carefully chosen. She prayed for "absent friends in all countries" when she was thinking of Morgan, knowing that Mademoiselle Marie could keep a secret but still feeling unequal to confessing the engagement. Louisa-Margaretta was the only person in their party who knew, and in spite of their argument, Judith felt certain that her friend would not give her away.

Morgan himself was a Quaker, so Judith knew that his prayers were different in manner but similar in substance.

She hoped that she still had a place in them. After such a long silence, her worries felt ever more serious, and she silently asked God to watch over him in Vienna.

9

Daria Ippolitovna's home was in a small street that Louisa-Margaretta would never have found on her own. The coachman seemed familiar enough with it, though, and she tried not to find herself surprised by the beauty of the painted homes near the Neva. She was accompanied by Susannah Cluett's maid, who had invited herself after helping Louisa-Margaretta dress. Louisa-Margaretta, who could hardly tell the woman that she was sneaking out against Madame Chatel and Mrs Cluett's wishes, pretended that she was happy for the assistance.

When Louisa-Margaretta and Masha the maid came into the entryway, Mary Josefa kissed Louisa-Margaretta with great affection then looked into her eyes with a combination of curiosity and certainty that made her blush.

"Masha," Mary Josefa said in French, "we do not require you at this time. Anya will see that you are shown to a place you may rest."

She then introduced Louisa-Margaretta to their host, Daria Ippolitovna. The young lady was very welcoming, but their greetings were overshadowed by the presence of Masha, who was looking like a trapped rabbit.

"Go on, then," said Louisa-Margaretta.

Louisa-Margaretta could tell that Masha struggled a bit with whether to disobey her mistress's instructions. Mrs Cluett, mother hen that she was, would no doubt have ordered Masha never to let Louisa-Margaretta out of her sight for a moment. Perhaps, having accompanied Louisa-Margaretta on a visit that the Cluetts had not wished her to make, Masha was already worried for her position. "I am happy, happy here with Miss Haddington," she managed to say in English.

Mary Josefa's English, though accented, was excellent. "Nonsense! Go, go. Have a rest. I won't let our dear Miss Haddington leave without you. Anya, show Masha to the tea room."

A slight young woman nodded, and Masha, clearly knowing when she had been beaten, followed her.

Mary Josefa gave a bright smile. Taking Louisa-Margaretta's arm, she showed her to a room that seemed as if it ought to be part of a gallery, with walls nearly covered by an immense number of paintings. Some of the portraits were fine, but their style was so given to excess that Louisa-Margaretta felt she might develop a headache. A young woman could not be pictured holding a single rose but rather a bouquet so large and healthy that it threatened to cover her entire figure. If there was a man on horseback, he was surrounded by cannons and smoke, only a part of his face visible. It was a most queer way to go about painting. Louisa-Margaretta, who had been firm for some time in her hatred for these artistic pursuits, found herself growing ever so slightly interested.

"I apologize for the walls," said Daria Ippolitovna. "I have been trying to find a home for all of the paintings, only they are so horrid and empty, nobody wants them."

"My dear," said Mary Josefa. "I am sure that some of your friends can be persuaded—"

"They can't," said Daria Ippolitovna firmly.

"We are traveling," said Louisa-Margaretta. "So I am afraid we cannot accept any paintings."

She heard a door opening then murmured greetings.

Daria Ippolitovna gave a shrug. "That will be Vladilena Maximovna now," she said. "But she will not take any. I have already asked her."

The three ladies went back to the door, where the doctor was briskly taking off her large cloak and hat. She handed these to Anya without a word then followed the little party to the dark room with all the paintings.

"Tell us what we must do, then," she said.

Daria Ippolitovna laughed for the first time. "All business with you, Lena," she said. "Just like at those other little gatherings. There is no time for chatter."

Louisa-Margaretta looked between them in confusion. "The other gatherings? The soirees, you mean?"

"Not the soirees, another sort of meeting," said Vladilena Maximovna. "Tell me, my friend. In England, you do not have serfs."

It was hardly a question. The doctor seemed very well informed, and Louisa-Margaretta found herself shockingly pleased to be referred to as a friend.

"No, we don't," she said. "Though Mama says that some of our children are treated worse than serfs." A ghost of a smile passed her lips when she thought of her mother. The one thing that Louisa-Margaretta and her mama had in common was that each of them always had a strong opinion about the topic at hand. And Mama was always going on about serfdom and slavery. Of course, dear Mama herself was the beneficiary of not only inherited wealth but the sort of riches that could only be gained by large machines replacing laborers, as Judith had once had the temerity to point out. But Judith believed Mama to be sincere in at least the most simple point, which was that some individuals ought not to assert the right of ownership over others. Whether she acknowledged that her hallboy's wages did not greatly improve his situation in life was less certain.

"Your mother sounds rather enlightened," said the doctor, her voice low. "Tell me, what are your own views on serfdom?"

Louisa-Margaretta sighed. "Look, I'm hardly a Russian, am I?" She knew that she could not tell the doctor that her only need was for a quick-thinking and discreet husband, but she was not going to sit and talk politics. "As far as I'm concerned, you may keep your serfs. Why should I tell you otherwise?"

The table next to her contained some rather pleasing wooden animals along with a large and inelegant boat that was plainly supposed to resemble Noah's ark. Louisa-Margaretta pushed at one of the little bears, amused to see that its facial expression resembled a sneer.

Vladilena Maximovna raised her chin. "I see. Not an opinion I expected from an Englishwoman who complains of the strictures placed on her own freedom, but perhaps you have not the experience to know otherwise."

Louisa-Margaretta looked down again at the miniatures. There was another set of little figurines. They appeared to be walking over to Noah's ark. Not every single one had a pair, and this disturbed her. For all her mysticism, Daria

Ippolitovna at least ought to know the story. But perhaps Russians told it differently.

"Tell me again about your meetings," she said.

But Daria Ippolitovna only shook her head. "If you don't think politics are for you, then the meetings certainly are not."

"Well, perhaps you ought to—" Louisa-Margaretta began to say.

"Ought to invite you? You'd find it dull," said the doctor.

Louisa-Margaretta had been going to suggest that she invite Judith. The latter seemed to have politics that were not so far from Daria Ippolitovna's. She was also in the habit of going on about how she ought to have the vote, along with all her neighbors. Louisa-Margaretta, who thought the House of Lords must be one of the dullest spectacles in England, found that she could not at all agree. But she remembered that she was cross with Judith and that she should stop having imaginary conversations with her.

"Please gather closer," said Mary Josefa. "Now, we must keep our minds from worldly matters and turn inwards, towards the divine. And yet this is also outwards."

Louisa-Margaretta tried to suppress a sigh. Mary Josefa was standing next to the fire, reaching out her hands. Daria Ippolitovna took one of them, Louisa-Margaretta the other.

"We must close the circle," said Daria Ippolitovna to Vladilena Maximovna. "Come, Lena."

When the doctor had grumbled her way in, Mary Josefa began to speak again. Her words were lilting, ambiguous, and yet strangely authoritative. She spoke of the many mysteries of this world and the next.

Louisa-Margaretta struggled to stay awake. When Anya came in to inquire about refreshments, Louisa-Margaretta and the doctor broke away. Louisa-Margaretta went to the window, where it was coolest, and blinked in the faint light. She had a murmured conversation with the doctor as Mary Josefa began telling Daria Ippolitovna about the surest signs of both spring and Godliness and how they needed to watch the fallow earth for the story of the resurrection.

"You ought to tell Daria Ippolitovna how much you despise all this," Louisa-Margaretta said. "You claim to be an old friend of the family, and yet you stand by while she is taken in with religious nonsense."

Louisa-Margaretta recalled her father, who had always been suspicious of genuinely religious people. He seemed to like Judith's father well enough but also took care to avoid him. And he never tolerated any talk of mystics, insisting that people who claimed to work miracles all used the same theatrical tricks.

But Louisa-Margaretta's companion only looked defeated as she shook her head. "I cannot bring her husband back," said the doctor. "Poor Dasha. I may heal, but I certainly cannot resurrect."

"And Mary Josefa can?"

"You heard her speaking about how our dead never leave us and calling on everyone to pray. As long as she keeps peddling such lies, I've no hope of dissuading Dasha."

"Then what shall you do?"

The doctor lowered her voice still more. "Hope that she leaves this city once she has gotten enough rubles from her benefactors. Indeed, her pilgrimage all over Europe ought to be continued in the spring, and if she can get horses, she might go to someone's country home and leave the rest of us to enjoy Petersburg."

Louisa-Margaretta frowned. She had heard very little about the royal family, and none of them had come as guests. Was this small gathering all she was to expect of the famous Mary Josefa? It seemed very dull indeed and now less likely to lead to a match than she had imagined. The little mystic did not have anything to say on the subject of marriage, and Louisa-Margaretta doubted that eligible bachelors would be taken in by her rhetoric. They might be interested in the charlatan's face, which was uncommonly beautiful, but would probably be bored to tears by all of her vague metaphors.

Taking her leave from the doctor, Louisa-Margaretta decided not to go back to the fireside at all but to slouch in a large chair and consider whether she should steal any of the miniatures. At least then, the whole journey would not have been for naught. She could not tolerate another hour of solemn prayers, and she was quite sure that nothing about the first one had shaken her.

But it was no use. That little elephant reminded her greatly of Isaac, her former fiancé. He was forever trotting out exemplars of lovely animals when she was cross with him, which was seldom enough. "Only think of elephants," he would say. "Can you believe that such creatures are walking the earth?"

Louisa-Margaretta always answered "no," because she could not. But she was charmed by his fascination with the natural world. It was childlike, in a sense.

She took one of the elephants and retreated to her chair, turning it over in her hand. Perhaps she would not steal it. If she told Daria Ippolitovna that she liked it, surely, it would be offered up as a gift. Such an offer, after all, was only polite.

Straightening, she realized that she was no longer alone in the room. "From the palace," a servant was saying in French. It was not Anya but someone in a royal livery. "She is very poorly, I am afraid."

Louisa-Margaretta stood at attention. A summons to the palace was a much more interesting matter, and she was gratified to see that Mary Josefa broke away from Daria Ippolitovna immediately.

"Of course," said the dark-haired woman, her face no longer suffused with a holy calm. "Bring me my coat, please! I shall leave immediately."

10

———

The Cluetts liked to rise early. It was another one of the intolerably English things about them. Though Louisa-Margaretta's family kept aristocratic hours, enjoying their breakfast only after the dining room was warm and every single dish cooked to perfection, still, Mama always went on about bracing morning walks and the dangers of idleness. Many of the Russians, Louisa-Margaretta had noted, were not at all ashamed to admit that they had risen after lunch. But Susannah Cluett seemed to delight in having her guests assembled around a bracing breakfast, where she apologized for the quality of the tea and went over the tasks laid before them for the day.

"Of course, Madame Chatel, you shall be working," she said. "We cannot interrupt you, only I hope on Sunday, you will take tea with us after church. Or, er, the Mass. Whatever ceremony."

"Thank you," said Madame Chatel, as easy as if she were already wielding her brush. "I shall look forward to it."

Louisa-Margaretta felt resentment rising in her. Once, when she had herself worked at a job like a common laborer, she had felt angry that so many of her hours were spoken for each day. And yet she found that she quite enjoyed having the obligation respected by others. Her brother Percival, who had been giving her all sorts of trouble at the time, was dispatched with phrases like "I would stay longer, but I must work" and "I mustn't be late; they'll be expecting me. Off with you, now." Even one of her suitors, who hardly ever let her alone, could occasionally be made to listen to reason when Louisa-Margaretta explained that her position was indispensable. She hadn't needed the money, but the employer had needed her, which was rather pleasant.

Now, apart from pretending to be ill, she had no escape from the likes of Susannah Cluett. And Louisa-Margaretta hated ladies who were always ill, fainting and carrying on. Though she herself had been feeling rather out of sorts for some time, from that most ancient of causes, her resolve not to appear weak and weary had only grown.

"There are more calls to be made," said Mrs Cluett delicately. "My dear young ladies, perhaps you will accompany me?"

"Of course," said Judith. "Marie, you'll join us, won't you?"

Louisa-Margaretta felt both pleased and angry that she had not been asked. Judith had not said so much as two words to her at the breakfast table.

"I was hoping you would come with me, Marie," she said. "My dear friend Miss, er, Ippolitovna has said I would be very welcome in her home again."

Once again, she cursed the Russians for having such strange names. She had no idea of Daria Ippolitovna's surname and could only remember others saying "Mademoiselle Daria" and "Dasha" in her presence. Apart from the servants, who called her Daria Ippolitovna to show respect.

The poor mademoiselle had no idea which way to turn. "Well, I would be happy to make calls, of course. But if your friend invited us both, Miss Haddington, I ought to go. Shouldn't I? I mean, if you said I would go."

Judith put a hand on the young lady's. "You may go where you wish, Marie."

Madame Chatel glared at both Judith and Louisa-Margaretta as if their quarrel were a conspiracy rather than a genuine disagreement. "You may not. This Daria Ippolitovna, I am to understand, is under the spell of some religious person."

"Mary Josefa," said Judith.

Louisa-Margaretta could tell that her friend was eager to defend anyone who would mock a pilgrim, even this mystic darling of the St Petersburg elite. Louisa-Margaretta did not mind hearing Mary Josefa's beliefs criticized, though she wanted to present a pretty picture for her hosts so it seemed that she could not refuse the invitation.

"Yes, we have hardly arrived here, and already, I hear that this woman has got half the town in thrall," said Madame Chatel. "Pretty words, and a pretty face to go along with them! That one knows more than she's telling, of that I am quite sure. You are not permitted to go and visit her, ma cher," she said to her daughter.

Louisa-Margaretta felt a frisson of annoyance. "Fine. I am more than happy to go on my own, and I will give our answer in such a way as to avoid offending Daria Ippolitovna."

She had sought to draw attention back to her Russian host, but she was not at all successful. Though Mrs Cluett murmured, "Yes, of course we should not wish her to be offended," Madame Chatel had not finished.

"You are also not permitted to go, Miss Haddington."

Louisa-Margaretta stared at her. Surely, the woman knew that the greatest danger in allowing a young woman to go out unchaperoned had already befallen her?

Madame Chatel, perhaps thinking on the same subject, spoke more gently. "Miss Haddington, I am not your mother."

Louisa-Margaretta gave a firm nod. "That is quite so. You are not."

"But I cannot allow you to make this sort of call. I am sure you will understand."

Judith had risen to her feet. "Perhaps another day," she said. "The weather is supposed to take a turn for the worse, I understand."

"Well, that is unfortunate," said Louisa-Margaretta. "Because it appears I shall have to walk."

Louisa-Margaretta spent only a few moments waiting for her coat, hat, and gloves. She permitted herself to wear boots, of course. She was not going to suffer through the snow. But as she stood, none of the ladies attempted to follow her.

Such fools, she thought to herself as she descended the stairs. She walked quickly past Gostiny Dvor, passing a group of women so small they looked like girls heading in the opposite direction. Ballerinas, most likely. Everyone spoke of the artistic delights of Petersburg, but they did not interest Louisa-Margaretta. Why would she sit and listen to others sing and dance? It had none of the luster of the real thing, the feeling she got from notes floating high over the heads of those watching her. Perhaps she should have been an actress herself.

Her breath floated out, clouding the air before her, as she released something that was almost a laugh. Acting! Mama would have locked her in a dungeon. Though her engagement with Isaac had seemed scandalous at the time, and many choices she had made since were hardly the picture of respectability, going on to the stage would be even worse than what she was doing now. Well-bred young ladies sometimes went out of the country if they found themselves "in difficulties" and wished to return, say, some months after. But there was no way to escape the scandal of acting. It was public by nature.

When she was about to turn a corner, Louisa-Margaretta heard two men arguing. Hoping to avoid their company, she shrank back before she came into their view. The men must also have been unmoving, because their voices did not change during their conversation.

"The country will always be in danger," said one of them. It took a moment for her to recognise the voice. It was the Prussian ambassador, and his French was so precise and measured that she found herself able to understand it.

There was another man speaking whose voice she could not identify. He spoke with an accent as well, but it sounded more heavily punctuated, perhaps in the manner of one who had grown up speaking Spanish.

"Those men have put themselves in danger," he said. "It is their conduct that haunts them, and that is only an effect of the power they have been given."

There was a pause. "The younger princes are not so horrid, surely," said the Prussian ambassador. "And the emperor, though he has his mistresses, tends to do things rather sequentially. He has the one, then he has the other, and it is all done with the utmost discretion."

"We do not know about him," said the other man,

though now he had lowered his voice. Louisa-Margaretta had trouble making it out, and she realised that even these foreign men had taken on the Russian custom of never speaking ill of the emperor. The snatches she heard puzzled her, just "his wife's affair" and "daughter by Okhotnikov." There was a longer pause, then the Prussian said something like "Why would a man not have a dozen or so bastard children if he were not to face any consequences for it? Not if he has enough of his own, that is."

Louisa-Margaretta felt her face grow red. She had tried not to think of the man who was the natural father of her child, but their phrasing had moved her. Indeed, he did not even know of Louisa-Margaretta's condition and would very likely never meet his natural child. With the protection and respectability afforded him by both his sex and his marriage, he could do as he pleased as a faraway spinster bore the grave consequences.

The voices died away. Louisa-Margaretta was very cold now, and as she trembled, she realized that her sense of direction had failed her. All of the buildings in the quarter where she now stood looked the same, and though she couldn't be far from the landmarks she knew, she had no idea which way to turn.

Louisa-Margaretta's courage was usually a matter of habit, though of late, it had been conspicuously absent. The knowledge that she was responsible for a small life within herself made her both more fearful and more determined. *Don't be a sapskull,* she told herself. This was no worse than being lost in the woods. She could simply find the nearest canal and follow it until she recognized her surroundings, the way she would with a little stream.

But no sooner had she made this resolution than a large, sharp object came hurtling towards her.

11

———

Judith was in the carriage, ready to start for Mary Josefa's, when she paused. The air was even colder than she had expected, and she was sure that Louisa-Margaretta could not be comfortable for long.

Leaning out the door, she asked the coachman to wait. But the street was quiet. She saw nobody walking about, and she had no sense of where her friend had gone. One person was walking quickly towards the Cluetts' home, but even under all his coats, she could see that he was a man.

In fact, he was a man of her acquaintance.

"Miss St Clair!" said Monsieur Zharkov, rushing over to the carriage. "How fortunate! I had just come to call on you, but I see you are going out."

"Yes," said Judith, the flush on her face not due entirely to worry for Louisa-Margaretta. "I have received an invitation, but I am concerned about my friend. Did you happen to see Miss Haddington on your way here?"

He shook his head. "I don't believe so. What sort of carriage was she in?"

"She was on foot, like yourself," said Judith, already beginning to shiver in the cold. She retreated to the interior of the carriage. Monsieur Zharkov, without being invited, followed her in.

Judith could hardly manage to look at him. She knew that the Russians had different feelings about propriety, generally speaking, but she hardly imagined that stretched to leaving an eager young gentleman with an unescorted lady in such a carriage, where they would be almost entirely hidden from public view.

Whatever Monsieur Zharkov's thoughts on the matter, though, he did not voice them. Instead, he asked Judith rapid questions about Louisa-Margaretta. Which way she had walked, where she intended to go, when she was expected to return.

"I let her go off without asking anything," said Judith, her voice catching. "She always goes outdoors when she is in a temper at home. But in this weather, I am very much afraid."

"Do not fear," said Monsieur Zharkov. "She may indeed be in an unenviable situation, your friend, but she cannot have gone far."

Judith clenched her hands together under her muff. She very much hoped that Monsieur Zharkov was not referring to the child Louisa-Margaretta was carrying when he spoke of her "unenviable situation." If Monsieur Zharkov knew this piece of information, it was soon to be widely known in Petersburg. The poor man, he could not seem to keep thoughts to himself, even secret ones.

He misunderstood her reaction and went to sit next to her, touching her arm in a manner that was overly familiar and not as reassuring as he must have meant it to be. "Oh, dear Miss St Clair, do not fear for your friend! You take the coach and look for her. Concentrate on the direction of the Neva, as you English visitors are always going to gawk at the river. I shall go in the opposite direction on foot."

And with that, he bounded out of the carriage and started down the street.

Though she was relieved that he was no longer sitting too close to her, Judith was horrified to see him out in the cold.

"Be careful!" she said to him, and he only laughed.

"You take care of yourself," he said. "Have no worries on my account. This cold is as nothing to me."

Judith stuck her head out to instruct the coachman. She managed to tell him, in Russian, that she wished to go to the Neva. He repeated the directions in French to make sure he had understood.

As the coach made its way down the street, Judith said a prayer for her friend. Louisa-Margaretta was a formidable huntress, and if she were on horseback in the chilly Derbyshire winter, Judith would not have worried. But the city of St Petersburg held unknown dangers, and she was very concerned that her friend would not know how to avoid all of them.

12

Louisa-Margaretta saw two things when she opened her eyes. First, the icicle that had come very close to striking her was now lying in pieces on the pavement. Second, a beautiful young woman, presumably having just rushed out of one of the residences, was standing over her with her arm outstretched.

"My dear," said the young woman. Her French was excellent. "Let me help you. You must come in."

"I—" Louisa-Margaretta managed to say. Her eyes felt most strange, as if under the hard lashes, she could hardly move them. "I thank you, yes." She took the proffered hand, scrambled to her feet, and followed the young woman to a modest door.

The home she entered was about the size of Daria Ippolitovna's, but that was where the similarities ended. Where the former home was eccentric, this place was quite cozy, clearly the sort of place where people actually lived.

Louisa-Margaretta found herself on a divan, wrapped in blankets, as the French speaker walked over to a samovar and brought back a beautiful cup of tea. As soon as she took the first sip, Louisa-Margaretta began coming to herself again. Her fingers, warmed from the fine china cup, were not going to fall off. She was not lost. She took another sip.

Louisa-Margaretta's rescuer, who had some long Russian name that seemed to contain not one but two family names after the patronymic, simply laughed at her attempts to pronounce it.

"You English ladies!" she exclaimed, not at all displeased. Her English, though not as good as her French, was still easy to understand. "I shall pick a simple English name. Ann. There! You may call me Ann."

The young woman who called herself Ann had a mother and three sisters, though Louisa-Margaretta noticed in a portrait that there was another sister as well. "Ann" delighted in giving all the sisters who were present English names, false ones, and so Louisa-Margaretta was told to call them Agnes, Augusta, and Alice. The lady of the house wished to be called by her proper name, but since Louisa-Margaretta did not come close to understanding it, she was forced to use only "madame" with her eyes lowered in an attempt to show respect. Somewhere in the surname had been "Kutuzova," she was sure of it. She would have to remember at least that in order to relay the whole thing to the Cluetts later.

"I did not think it would be so impossible to walk in the Russian winter," Louisa-Margaretta confessed to Ann, who squeezed her arm in sympathy but gave a merry laugh.

"Oh, how my father would have laughed at what you just said, Miss Haddington." Ann sighed before relaying Louisa-Margaretta's remarks to her sisters and mother. They all laughed except for Augusta, who wiped away a tear. Just then, all her sisters were embracing her, some of them crying as well.

Louisa-Margaretta wondered if they were mad. "And your father? Is he from home?"

"He died a year ago," said Ann. "Oh, you did not know? I am sorry. I forget you are not Russian."

"I'm very sorry," said Louisa-Margaretta.

Ann nodded sagely. "Well, we have his salary, each of us, so it is more than most can boast of. But we miss him terribly, of course."

Augusta, having got over her crying spell, went to Louisa-Margaretta's side. "Miss Haddington," she said shyly. "Why have you come to St Petersburg?"

Louisa-Margaretta thought of dissembling. But in this company of warmhearted ladies, she felt more at home than she had since leaving Derbyshire. "Well, I am looking for a husband," she said. "My fortune is large, so he can be poor, but I should greatly prefer not to marry an idiot."

The ladies all began to laugh together, and Augusta suggested that Louisa-Margaretta find them all husbands as well. Apparently, though not all of the ladies were perfectly young, none of them was married. But the lady of the house was not at all amused. She came over and spoke to Ann in rapid Russian, most of which the latter did not translate.

Ann only patted Louisa-Margaretta's hand. "It is good to choose well," she said. "Our parents had a good marriage, but many others do not turn out at all."

"Indeed," said Louisa-Margaretta. "I have heard that Konstantin Pavlovich, the brother of your emperor, does not see a great deal of his wife. He has banished her across a continent! Apart from this, I am open to nearly any sort of husband."

Ann looked apprehensive for a moment. She was silent as her mother spoke.

"What does she say?" asked Louisa-Margaretta.

"That sending his wife away is the best thing he has ever done, the best treatment he has ever given a woman," said Ann, reddening.

Seeing as the ladies were obviously all uncomfortable, Louisa-Margaretta decided to continue asking them about marriage. It could hardly do any harm. "Well, at any rate, he is already married. Is there anyone you would recommend as a husband?"

One of the younger girls, the one they were calling Augusta, grinned. "Not Russian man," she said proudly.

An older sister corrected her. "Not *a* Russian man."

"Perhaps a French one," said the sister who had been called Agnes with a sly grin. "And maybe one who is musical?"

Louisa-Margaretta felt offended then pleased. Apparently, even these ladies whom she had never met had heard rumours about her performance with Mr Solier. She had assumed that he was unaffected, as he did not seek her out during the event at the palace. But perhaps her suit was not hopeless in that direction. After all, when he was not obligated to pay every attention to members of the royal family, he seemed to quite like speaking with Louisa-Margaretta.

"Tell me more about such a man," said Louisa-Margaretta, beginning to smile.

But another man interrupted. A servant brought a large man, his face pink from cold, into the cozy little room, and the spell was broken.

"Monsieur Zharkov," said the matriarch formally. "Do sit down and take tea with us."

"Thank you," he said in Russian, but Louisa-Margaretta did not catch the rest of his statement. He sat and turned a stern glance on her.

"You have caused your friends great worry," he said. "I

hope you were planning on sending word to poor Miss St Clair? Even now, she is somewhere near the Neva, hoping to find you."

Louisa-Margaretta felt a moment's guilt, but she was not about to show any weakness in front of Monsieur Zharkov. She had gotten a bit lost, perhaps, but it was no reason for him to treat her so rudely.

"How did you know I was here?" snapped Louisa-Margaretta, glancing towards the frosty windows. Nobody ought to have known.

He shrugged. "I am sure that in England, you also have gossip," he said, standing. "Well, you seem well enough."

He called for his coat, and when it did not appear instantly, he began to stride back towards the passageway. Only Ann stopped him, and the servant came. As soon as he had fastened the coat and put on his hat, he was nearly at the door.

"Wait for me," said Louisa-Margaretta.

"I cannot," he said. "After a time, someone will come from the Cluetts' to bring you back. For the moment, I have an urgent errand to attend to."

13

———

After what felt like an age on the banks of the Neva, Judith asked the coachman to go back to the Cluetts'. She was pained to admit failure, all while she was letting poor Mary Josefa down, but it could not be helped. They had gone so far that they would have come across Louisa-Margaretta.

Judith very much hoped that her friend had not had any sort of fainting spell. She knew that this tender stage, for a woman in her friend's condition, could be delicate. Louisa-Margaretta, who had never been prone to ill health of any sort, would not know how to protect herself. By the time they neared the Cluetts', Judith was sick with worry.

Then she saw Monsieur Zharkov. "All is well," he said. "Your friend is an inconsiderate ninny, but she is not hurt."

Judith herself felt weak, and she held tight to the windowsill of the carriage. "Where is she?"

"With a family of my acquaintance. She is not far. We can go and fetch her now if you like."

He invited himself into the carriage, and Judith was so uncomfortable that she insisted on going into the Cluetts' to fetch someone else who might accompany them. But because Madame Chatel and Mrs Cluett were both put out by all the chaos that Louisa-Margaretta's rash actions had caused, in the end, only Marie ended up joining them.

"Could you tell us of the family who is sheltering our friend, Monsieur Zharkov?" said Marie.

The young man, whose face was becoming less red in the comfortable seat of the carriage, looked out the tiny window and shook his head. "They are a family of the first order. The Golenishcheva-Kutuzova ladies are the daughters of our great general, Mikhail Illarionovich Golenishchev-Kutuzov."

Marie's brow furrowed in confusion, but Judith was able to explain.

"He chased the French out of Russia after they invaded, under Napoleon Bonaparte," she said. "Your mother will have told you about him."

Marie sank more deeply into her seat. "Yes, quite," she said, plainly miserable.

Judith felt for the young woman. Poor Marie did not share her mother's hatred of Napoleon Bonaparte, and she had little interest in the wars that had shaped her entire life. But she could never avoid hearing of them, especially not in Russia, which was still reeling from the shock of the invasion and the national pride that had burst forth on Napoleon's defeat.

"I have heard of his daughters," said Judith. "There are several, I believe, but he had no sons."

"Yes, most unfortunate," said Monsieur Zharkov, his customary good cheer returning as he thought of the old general. "Such a man, and he had only daughters!"

"Some daughters are quite as courageous as sons," said Judith carefully. She would have liked to add that Louisa-

Margaretta had more strength and stubbornness than any of her brothers, but she knew that Monsieur Zharkov was not disposed to think well of the young lady who had charged recklessly into the Russian winter.

"Perhaps in England," said Monsieur Zharkov stoutly. "But in Russia, few men are dear General Kutuzov's equal. No men, really, though it is a shame that he had no son to carry on his name and his legacy."

"Yes," said Judith blandly. She could see that Monsieur Zharkov, as a military man, was not likely to be interested in her treatise on the rights of women. So she remained silent until they reached the home that had once belonged to the general. Judith saw that his wife and daughters seemed quite ensconced there, and she hoped that whichever male relative now owned the place would be happy to let them stay.

Though the family could hardly have been more welcoming, and Louisa-Margaretta herself was happy to stay, Judith was uncharacteristically firm. She wanted her friend in the carriage, and she wanted to take her back to the Cluetts' home. Immediately.

14

______

When they came back to the Cluetts', it did not matter that Louisa-Margaretta could not recall the name of her rescuers. Mrs Cluett and Madame Chatel had already heard the news.

"How?" said Louisa-Margaretta faintly, and Judith shook her head.

"Word travels," she said. "The same as it does back home."

When Louisa-Margaretta was settled in her bed, with only Judith near her, she closed her eyes for a moment. How glorious it would be to sleep and to forget everything that had happened during the day! Yet that would also be an abdication of her duty. She ought to tell Judith about the argument she had overheard between the two men. They had their own ideas about the attacks, and the part about the man and his children, while disturbing, intrigued Louisa-Margaretta.

But Judith would not hear of it.

"You need to rest," she said. "And I must send for a

doctor. You had us all worried." She moved as if she would take Louisa-Margaretta's hand then looked away.

Louisa-Margaretta noticed that her friend was pale. "Don't be an old woman," she said, stoutly enough that she hoped she would not betray her own tiredness. "I am perfectly well."

"But in your condition—"

"In my condition, I need a decent cup of tea and a rest. I can't abide this Russian tea. It's so strong we could use it to scrub the floors."

There was a faint smile on Judith's face. "Have you ever scrubbed a floor, then?"

"I have, thank you. And more than once. Only when we were both working, of course. One of those terrible young ladies puked all over the floor. To spite me, I am certain, as she seemed well enough afterwards."

Judith was laughing. "That is not so unusual when one is sick."

Louisa-Margaretta smiled then closed her eyes again. She could rest now that her friend was not cross with her. The details of her fury with Judith faded away, and though she did not wish to admit it, she was relieved that Judith seemed to have forgiven her all of her outbursts and petulance.

Of course Judith was forgiving, but she was never inclined to forget her aim. "I will have Mrs Cluett send for a doctor," she said. "Truly, Louisa-Margaretta. I know not what dangers—"

"If there are any, it is too late to do anything about them now," said Louisa-Margaretta. She was surprised that she felt a pang of fear herself. She had spent so many weeks agonizing over the thought of being a mother that the idea of laying down this mantle filled her with a sorrow that was poignant and surprising.

Judith was not going to be placated. "But someone knowledgeable, at least. I can ask Vladilena Maximovna, your friend!"

Louisa-Margaretta sank into her pillows. "If my condition worsens, then I shall allow you to summon her. If tea and a bit of a rest are all I need, then we shall look no further. Agreed?"

Judith had grabbed one edge of the blanket, and she was worrying it between her fingers. Louisa-Margaretta tore it away.

"I'm sorry, Louisa-Margaretta," said Judith. "But I cannot keep myself from feeling concerned, not when you were out in such cold."

"Well, you ought to be concerned, because I am no nearer to finding a husband than I was when we came," snapped Louisa-Margaretta. "I would prefer not to hide out in the country all spring like some shamed hussy."

Judith's expression was pained. "Surely, not every woman who finds herself with child ought to be treated as such. Indeed, your mother has often said, and I know my father passionately agrees with her—"

"Judith," said Louisa-Margaretta. Goodness, the last thing she wanted to think about was her mother or her friend's sanctimonious father! Judith, who usually read her friend's thoughts perfectly well, ought to have known this. "I don't want words of wisdom. I want an eligible young man! If I marry before the year is out, there will be gossip, but my child will have a father."

Judith snapped to attention. Louisa-Margaretta was well aware that this was the first time she had spoken so frankly of the problem that had occupied them for months. She was going to be a mother, and if she did not prepare, she would be in an immeasurably worse situation. She no longer felt certain that she wished the baby to be whisked away from her, to be given some Russian name and a passel of false siblings. It had seemed very reasonable to her once, as she knew how much certain couples longed for children. But would she not long for the little one herself? Why should she act like she was one of those desperate women, ready to leave a bundle on the stairs of a foundling hospital, when she had no fear of the type of poverty that they faced? She cared less about her good name than before, though she had to admit the possibility that her parents would leave her to starve if she had a child out of wedlock.

A husband it was, then. At least she would have help.

"I understand," Judith said, clasping her hands together as she thought. "I shall help you find someone. I promise. Give me more time to arrange this party, and I shall see to it that you meet several eligible young men before the end of the night."

15

———

The evening of the Christmas party came, and it was fair and cold. Judith found, for the first time, that she was rather heartened by the dark evenings. She had found them quite gloomy at first, but when the home was lit with candles in anticipation of a true English Christmas, it looked almost perfect. Judith never would have taken herself for a provincial before, but she found herself homesick for the sort of Christmas she had always known. True, in a clergyman's household, the holiday meant a great deal of work. As a child, Judith had been forced to listen to her father's tedious superior, Mr Lewis, berating his congregants for their poor attendance in the parish church. But still, there was a certain spirit about the whole thing, all very different from the Russian customs. As the Orthodox Christmas would come later, none of the observance seemed the same, and Judith was thankful for the opportunity to recall her own treasured Christmas traditions.

Of course, as the cosmopolitan group of guests began filling the Cluetts' residence, it felt less and less like an

English Christmas. For one thing, in spite of the excellence of the cooking, Mrs Cluett had allowed herself to be convinced that it would be offensive to the Russian guests if they did not serve local delicacies. Judith did not love the taste of the Russian cheeses or that of the stinging, bready kvass on her tongue.

In fact, she never would have accepted a glass at all were it not for Monsieur Zharkov. He arrived at the party just as it was beginning then proceeded to give her an account of his day walking on the ice of the bay. He had been looking for good fishing, only he had not found it. Fishing on a lake in winter was an accepted, reasonable pastime. The bay was so vast that one man walking on ice in a shallow part could not expect to see a great deal by way of fish.

"I wonder why you try it, then," said Judith, gently. "Surely, there are fish to be got here in the city."

"But that is not fishing, not at all! Pah. To stand on a bridge in summer, dangling a line into the water, hoping for an easy meal? It is a silly thing. And making little holes to feast on canal fish, no, that is even more ridiculous."

"I meant fish that one can *buy*," said Judith. "From a fish-monger. For ready money."

She could not say why, but she felt inclined to tease Monsieur Zharkov. And she knew that while his circumstances were not the grandest of all their guests, they would certainly run to sending a servant to purchase fish for his table.

"Ah, no!" he said. "For shame. A man ought to eat what he hunts and kills himself."

"And dig his own vegetables, I suppose?"

Judith felt that she might have insulted him, but he only laughed. "I do not object to digging, but I do object to vegetables. I'm afraid that twisting a carrot is not at all the same as stalking game, and the flavor is certainly far less enticing."

Judith laughed then stopped herself. She looked about for Louisa-Margaretta, her usual response when she was receiving unwanted attention from a young man. The whole evening had been in service of Louisa-Margaretta's search for a beau, and Judith had allowed Monsieur Zharkov's conversation to distract her.

It's more than conversation, it's flirtation, she told herself, feeling a prick of conscience. But no sooner had she found her friend, closely followed by Monsieur Zharkov, than the dancing began.

"You must all join me for a mazurka!" said Monsieur Zharkov, his eyes gleaming. His French sounded somehow exaggerated, as if he were trying to speak with twice the accent of any Parisian. "All of you. Miss, if I could ask for this dance?"

"Of course," said Louisa-Margaretta. "Of course, I am still learning the steps. Dear Miss St Clair, I am sure you know them well enough!"

Even if Judith had tried to refuse, Monsieur Zharkov would have insisted in his eagerness. Judith was not sure if he understood her reluctance and wished her to move past it or if she simply had not been clear enough with him. As she had been raised to value politeness over everything apart from godliness, it was sometimes difficult for Judith to express herself firmly. For example, she ought to say that she had absolutely no intention of dancing, but she could only manage "I don't know the steps very well yet, no."

Monsieur Zharkov only grinned. "Then you need a partner who is a true leader!"

He was a leader, Judith would have to grant him that. As the music began, she took her place across from him, and she saw Louisa-Margaretta still sparkling with youth and vigor as she joined a new young man. Judith remembered inviting him. Mr Autin was aristocratic, to be sure, but did he wish for an English wife? And was he the sort of man who would understand the delicate situation in which she found herself?

As the music began, Judith could not help fretting over her friend. She remembered various instances of her parents refusing to condemn couples who married when the lady was clearly with child and knew that in more than one of those instances, the father of the child had not been the prospective husband. Though such gossip really ought not to have reached her ears, it was all part of growing up in a village as well as being a confidante of her mother's.

"People say that children are holy, but then they condemn a woman with child as being not holy at all," she remembered her mother saying. "Don't even think of believing such nonsense, Judith. Every child is a gift, and the circumstances of others' lives are sometimes beyond our imagination."

At the time, Judith had resented it and complained. "We see all sorts of people, Mama. Do you really think I am so naive as to accept the judgments of the wagging tongues?"

Mama had stroked her hair. "I did not mean to insult you, dearest. I only meant that you are young. Keep your mind as open as it is now, and you will please God. And be happier yourself, I dare say, by keeping your heart gentle and kind."

Over the years, Judith had come to understand that her mother was correct. She had heard many women condemned, and often the harshest voices were those of other women. She had also heard men praised for making ugly pronouncements about what they would do if their wife strayed and how they would not think of allowing their sons to wed any "girl" who was not innocent. These were oftentimes the same men who felt that they and their sons could behave as they pleased. Innocence and virginity were not to be prized or expected in men.

The young man dancing with Louisa-Margaretta was handsome enough, to be sure. And he was certainly in good spirits. But would he accept a wife who was already with child? Worse, if Louisa-Margaretta did not tell him, was there any chance he would hurt her when he discovered the secret? Or harm the child?

Judith shuddered. She knew that she ought to finish dancing the mazurka, but it seemed interminable, all of this hopping and turning. Something about the room made her uneasy. The evening was wearing on, all sorts of drinks were being served, and the tones of the voices had risen proportionally. There was gaiety, to be sure, but she found something ominous in all the noise. Some part of her mind was sounding a warning, and she ought to listen.

The realization came to her only as the dance was ending. It was the esteemed royal guests that Mrs Cluett had worked so very hard to welcome.

One of them was missing.

16

Louisa-Margaretta did not wish to listen to her friend at first. "Look," she said. "Some members of the royal family might wish for a bit of privacy. In fact, I have heard something to that effect."

Louisa-Margaretta hoped she would not have to spell such things out to her friend. Though upstanding Judith was surely still a maiden, she was no stranger to the temptations of time alone with one's beloved. Though perhaps Judith would find it rather strange to seek out someone who was not the light of one's soul, rather only a fleeting lover. That would seem scandalous to her.

Judith was still shaking her head. She had not been able to get rid of Monsieur Zharkov. In fact, she was so often with him that Louisa-Margaretta was beginning to feel she had misjudged her friend. Was Judith truly still engaged to Cousin Morgan? She had seemed happy enough earlier, eating little birdlike bites of the English refreshments and laughing away as the bold and cheerful Russian told his stories. The man was taken with her, that much was certain, but Louisa-Margaretta had been rather surprised that Judith was giving him so much encouragement.

"It cannot be," said Judith firmly. "I can feel that there is something wrong. Vladilena Maximovna is just there, if you can fetch her."

Though Judith's statements were polite, her tone was firm, and Louisa-Margaretta did not bother to hide her sigh. The young man she had been dancing with was now dancing with a Russian young lady. A girl who was pretty, and probably much younger. And one who understood this strange society in which they were all forced to move.

Louisa-Margaretta forced her way through the crowd, which she knew Judith had not wished to do.

"So very sorry," she said, not bothering to pretend any such thing. "My friend Miss St Clair wishes to speak with you, Doctor. I believe some poor soul is indisposed."

Vladilena Maximovna, who had been fanning herself with a sour face, came to attention. "Well, then."

Soon, the four of them were ascending the stairs. They knew the person they were seeking but not what they should expect to find. Louisa-Margaretta was still arguing that any individual who snuck away from such a gathering ought not to be interrupted, and for very good reason. She knew that when her parents threw a party, certain unacknowledged pairs of men and women might absent themselves. So long as neither of the parties was an unmarried young lady, everyone tended to pretend not to notice the absence, though Louisa-Margaretta knew that the married ladies would be sending each other rather significant looks.

Of course, some people would always be embarrassed by this reality. Monsieur Zharkov only cleared his throat, catching the doctor's eye before he looked away. The Russian lady slowed on the stairs, thinking on Louisa-

Margaretta's words, then nodded and began ascending them even more briskly.

"Right. We should not waste our time. When help is needed, it should come right away. Or we could well be too late. Which bedroom, then?"

It was rather direct, even for Louisa-Margaretta. "I'm sorry?"

"Which is the bedroom? Never mind," she said. For now, they all heard the groaning.

Louisa-Margaretta, who had already begun to blush, turned red at the sound. It was just as she thought, then, and they all ought to turn around and pretend not to know anything about it. She tried not to look at any other members of the party, but Monsieur Zharkov and the doctor were nearly sprinting ahead. The room was not locked.

But the sight inside was more shocking than any of them could have imagined.

17

A man was on the floor. He was making inhuman sounds, twisted with pain, and was most clearly injured.

Judith had never had a weak stomach when it came to blood. Around Wycliff Castle, the joke was always that Judith could tolerate human blood and Louisa-Margaretta could tolerate animal blood. Judith would hide her face if someone had shot the wrong part of a fox. The poor, wounded animal! She would invariably call Louisa-Margaretta to finish the job each time there was a hunting incident in which the poor beast did not die. Whereas when some young St Clair brother cut himself playing outdoors, as often happened, Judith was quick to clean and dress the wound. And Louisa-Margaretta would rather vanish than be troubled by others' injuries.

But even Judith could not move towards the man at first. He was not only bleeding, he seemed to be actively disintegrating before them.

"A knife," said the doctor, kneeling next to him. She

spoke to the man in Russian. Judith could hear the words, guttural and snappish. "Be still."

The poor man was not still but stopped writhing in pain. "Get his jacket off" was the next command from the doctor, issued in French. Louisa-Margaretta was standing by the door, but Judith and Monsieur Zharkov grabbed the arms of the man's jacket, wrenching it off him. They worked together as if in a strange sort of sport, and Judith was surprised that they did not need to speak in order to understand the next move. The jacket was removed. Each of them grabbed one side of the fellow's shirt. Judith pulled, Monsieur Zharkov pulled harder, and it tore down the middle.

The doctor took a blanket from the bed then produced a bottle. Vodka. A bedroom seemed a strange place for such a spirit. She looked as if she were going to clean the wound, but instead, she lifted her fingers up to Judith's head.

Judith gasped as her hairpins scraped her skin. Vladilena Maximovna was pulling at the turban Judith had placed so carefully over her thin hair, wrenching it away. Soon, the doctor had the turban completely off, and it took her only a moment to unwind it, though there remained a little knotted bit at the end that she could not get undone. The doctor began yanking the turban around the man's arm, wrapping it quickly but with care.

"Tighter, tighter," Judith heard her mutter in Russian. "*Tak.*"

Judith had thought that the man's torso was injured, but she saw that he had been stabbed in his arm. Perhaps he had been moving his entire body because he could not stand the pain. But now, having lost a good deal of blood, he would be too weak to fight.

Now, the doctor began to clean the wound, which set the

man to moaning again. Without being asked, Monsieur Zharkov produced a handkerchief, and Judith found herself doing the same.

"Your handkerchiefs, Louisa-Margaretta," she said to her friend, who was staring at the door and looking rather wobbly.

"I don't want them ruined," said Louisa-Margaretta, her pale face narrowed against giving up her fine linens.

"We need something clean," said Judith. "We will get through ours in no time. There's a lot of blood."

"No need to put it like that," snapped Louisa-Margaretta, but she handed over her handkerchiefs. "Save these if you can. I'll send a servant for something else."

She left, shoving the door shut behind her, and Judith stayed. She was trembling with the excitement, but because the man seemed to be recovering, she was able to lean against the door and begin to take in the meaning of the soft conversation.

For Vladilena Maximovna was interrogating the man. There was no other word for it. Their Russian was rapid but simple, and Judith understood the exchange.

"Who told you to come here?"

He did not answer.

Monsieur Zharkov, frowning, asked the question again. "Who was it? Who did this?"

"There was a message. A lady wished to meet me here," the injured man said weakly.

"Which lady?" said Monsieur Zharkov.

"How should I know? There's a blindfold there, by the mirror."

Judith saw Monsieur Zharkov's shoulders fall as the doctor shook her head. He was a man of military training, after all, and she was sure that he could spot the risks in this plan.

"So you came to a room, based on a message, to meet a woman you may have never met before? And you did not remove the blindfold?" Monsieur Zharkov, though his tone had been respectful, was so shocked that he began to sound impudent.

"What if she were ugly?" came the querulous answer. "Usually, when they ask you not to look, there's a reason."

Monsieur Zharkov looked carefully at the man's wounded arm. The doctor had cleaned it, but the blood was now soaking into her clothes. "Who gave you the message?"

When no response was forthcoming, he scowled. "This good lady here is trying to save your life and your arm. Without her, you may die or be crippled."

The man looked as if he wished to spit on both of them. "Nobody gave it to me. I found it in my pocket after one of the dances."

Monsieur Zharkov regarded him carefully.

"Do you still have it?"

The man nodded at the fire. "Course not. Nobody keeps that sort of thing. It isn't, you understand, of a sentimental nature."

"Well," said Monsieur Zharkov, making an effort to speak his accented French again. "Vladilena Maximovna seems to have saved your life, but we must transport you to the palace immediately. Miss St Clair, if you would?"

Judith started. "Of course, of course." But she lingered at the door, listening to the rest of the conversation.

"I do not like to move you," said the doctor. "But if I can dress the wound first, I agree that we ought to get you to the palace. While you are here, everyone in this home is in danger."

This seemed to disturb the man more than anything else that had been said. "Did you see the woman who did this? Did she?"

"It might not have been a woman," said Monsieur Zharkov, adding "your excellency" somewhat belatedly.

"Of course it was a woman! I might not have seen her, but I'll be damned if it was a man."

"Why would that be?" said Monsieur Zharkov, but the royal made no answer.

It came to Judith that the entertainment the man had expected from the "maiden" might have commenced, at least in part, before the attack. If that were the case, he was sure to insist that the person who had tried to kill him was a woman, not a man who had posed as such in order to seduce and murder a member of the royal family.

Louisa-Margaretta came back in the door and began tugging at Judith's wrist. "They're coming up the stairs," she whispered.

Monsieur Zharkov had the same thought. He and the doctor exchanged glances.

"Send them off," she said harshly, her Russian quick and guttural. "They can't be seen here. And you," she said to her patient. "Don't you dare think of bringing the names of these young ladies into your account."

Judith shoved the dressings Louisa-Margaretta had brought at the doctor. Monsieur Zharkov put one hand on her back and another on her shoulder, steering her to the door with the familiarity of a lover. If she had not been afraid to be caught in that room, she would have worried about Louisa-Margaretta's teasing. The two of them had hardly made it to their bedchamber when they heard the commotion of all sorts of royal retainers.

"Oh, Louisa-Margaretta," she said. "How perfectly awful.

I wish we had never gone along with this scheme. To bring the villain here, to the Cluetts' home!"

Louisa-Margaretta went to the mirror, adjusting one of her curls. It was as if she believed the evening might still be saved, that she might float down the stairs and ask another handsome young Frenchman to dance.

"I suppose you ought to trust your instincts, Judith," she said slowly. "They probably saved that prince tonight, along with the doctor's ministrations. Doesn't sound like he's keen to give women any credit for such things, though, so if you're expecting a medal of valor, you may be waiting for some time."

"I'm not," said Judith, joining her friend at the mirror. She tried to fix her wispy hair then gave up. Without the turban, she looked a fright. But unlike Louisa-Margaretta, she knew that the festivities were well and truly over. "But I am expecting to catch a murderer. In fact, I believe it's essential."

Louisa-Margaretta twisted one of her curls around her finger, sighing. She powdered her nose then took out cream for her hands. They were already pale, but with the cream, they looked as white as the snow outside. "Whyever would it be, Judith? Whoever was in that room tonight did not kill the prince."

"They would have," said Judith, insistent. "And do you not see what this individual is doing?"

"Running around, posing as a woman to entrap silly men who take no care for their own safety? A letter from an unnamed sender, telling him to meet, which he burned! Of all the foolishness."

"No," said Judith. "They are working their way up, hurting every single one of Emperor Paul's children. And I do not believe they will stop until they have murdered the very emperor."

"Who is not here at present," said Louisa-Margaretta, frowning at her friend.

"No," said Judith, her voice trembling. "He is in Vienna, like— He is at the congress. And if he is assassinated, the fragile peace our world has found may well fail at once."

18

"Oh, not the emperor, I am quite sure," said Susannah Cluett.

Louisa-Margaretta was rather pleased to see that their hostess was taking her side. Judith's idea was too far-fetched, after all.

"But, if you please," said Judith. Her eyes had flickered back to Louisa-Margaretta, who was annoyed by the thoughts that Judith would not admit to. She would be thinking of how precarious their place was with the Cluetts. If they turned out to be difficult guests, they could just be ordered to leave. After all, Madame Chatel had been invited for her obvious artistic gifts. She had used all her charm in explaining that Judith and Louisa-Margaretta were there as companions for her daughter, dear Marie, but it would not be surprising if the Cluetts were not quite convinced. After all, Marie Chatel was hardly a bosom friend of either of them—any fool could see that. Louisa-Margaretta had spent most of the time trying to ignore that mopish young girl, and though Judith had been kind, it must have been obvious that the two elders were much fonder of each other than they were of the homesick girl.

Judith was making a mare's nest of her explanation. "The youngest son was not killed, and neither was the next after him. But can you not see that this was only a run of good luck? They did not know, perhaps, that an able doctor could save Prince Nicholas's life. But in the next incident, luck may not be with us."

"Your conception of the next incident appears rather vague," said Mr Cluett, his bushy eyebrows knitted together in concentration. "When do you suppose it shall happen? And do you think this attacker is going after all the emperor's siblings or only the brothers?"

Judith was studying her shoes. "I don't know," she said, her voice soft. "I mean, I think they all ought to be warned. But if the aim is to bring down the throne, it makes sense that it would be all of them, doesn't it? The daughters are either unwed or have marriages of great import."

"Marriages are just marriages," said Louisa-Margaretta. "What import could they have that would make the wives worth killing along with the husbands?" She could hear how rude her tone was but could not keep herself from speaking. As much as she wished for a marriage, chiefly for her child's benefit, the old part of her that had fought such strictures for a decade was not yet completely dormant.

Judith was staring in horror. Though the diplomats hosting them would have been better placed to explain the importance of strategy in royal alliances, which Louisa-Margaretta did at least partly understand, Judith spoke first.

"Princess Anna Pavlovna, sister of the two young men, was supposed to marry *Napoleon Bonaparte!*" she cried. "Imagine if that had happened, how many things would be different! The discussions now taking place in Vienna could not happen, for how would Emperor Alexander think it right to take Poland from his brother-in-law?"

"Perhaps Napoleon Bonaparte would not have burned down the capitol city of *his* brother-in-law," said Louisa-Margaretta tartly. "And a very good thing that would have been too."

"Ladies," said Mr Cluett. "I thank you for the warning that you bring us. But I am afraid my wife and I have noticed a rather different set of consequences that may spring from these unfortunate events."

Judith stiffened.

Louisa-Margaretta felt herself clenching her hands, but she forced a small smile. "What would that be?"

"Your names are mentioned in conjunction with both," said Mrs Cluett. "It would be impossible to overlook that, in both instances, you were some of the earliest, er, the first to see the unfortunate gentlemen." She finished the sentence quickly.

"What does that mean?" asked Judith.

Louisa-Margaretta looked over at her rather sharply. She did not like the tremor she had heard in Judith's voice.

"It means that you should not even think of speaking of these incidents," said Mr Cluett. "Alas, our plan to distract the city of St Petersburg with Christmas festivities only provided cover for another attack. You must both avoid large gatherings while this maniac is still on the loose."

"So that he can attack and perhaps kill someone else?" said Louisa-Margaretta, glaring at them. "You would have us do nothing to help?"

At this, Susannah Cluett gave a rather sharp titter. "You, help? Please, Miss Haddington. You are our guest, but do not think you can help when it comes to Russian court intrigue. You could not possibly be so naive."

Louisa-Margaretta's eyes flashed with violence, real and imagined. "I can assure you, we are in a better position to help than you might realize. In fact, in the past—"

Judith interrupted her. Louisa-Margaretta knew that Judith hoped to keep her from explaining that they had gotten to the bottom of a great many murders in the past. Though keeping this secret rankled, Louisa-Margaretta knew that Judith was right. They had much better pretend to be docile young ladies, a role that was familiar for Judith, who cleared her throat delicately.

"Of course, we shouldn't wish to alarm anyone. But will it not appear strange if we avoid gatherings? After all, at this time of year, there seems to be a beautiful little party nearly every evening."

Mr Cluett shook his head. "What my wife may refer to is the very real danger that lurks beneath the beauty." He lowered his voice to a whisper. "I assume you both have heard how Emperor Alexander came to power?"

When Louisa-Margaretta shook her head, Judith nodded. "I can tell you later," she said to her friend, and the Cluetts both looked as if they approved. Louisa-Margaretta was irritated to once more be forced to bow to Judith's superior understanding of politics. Had she known they would bear witness to failed assassination attempts, Louisa-Margaretta would have learned more about Russia before they began their journey.

"We cannot stay in," she said. "I am quite sorry, but for every event! You tell us not to draw attention to ourselves, but if we never go out, the whole city shall wonder at it."

Susannah Cluett frowned. "It would look rather odd," she said. "Here is how we shall plan it. I will accompany you for the small ones, but when there is an event with the whole city, we shall find a way to avoid it."

"No," said Louisa-Margaretta.

Judith, who was nodding, attempted to quiet her friend. "Louisa-Margaretta, what choice do we have? It's not as if we can go to some other city until the danger is past. We are forced to stay in St Petersburg, so we may as well make the best of things."

Mr Cluett nodded solemnly. "If ever I felt the danger was too great, it would be quite hard for all of you to get even as far as Moscow. But perhaps you could go to a country house for a time if we could think of a way to accomplish this."

"Yes," said his wife. "That is what we ought to do if things get even worse."

He squeezed her hand. "I did tell you, dear."

She looked away. "He wanted me to stay in England with our children. But whither thou goest and all that."

Louisa-Margaretta knew that Judith had always loved the story of Naomi and Ruth. And indeed, Judith gave the couple a warm and syrupy smile.

Louisa-Margaretta had never liked the story, especially when it was told by her mother, who certainly would not have done any such thing for her own mother-in-law. And Louisa-Margaretta hated the idea of being shut up in a country house. To reach her time there and be forced to beg even more assistance from the Cluetts? If she married soon, she could escape this insufferable couple.

Only, to do so, it appeared necessary that a murderer be caught. That should not be too terrible.

She stood. "I had already promised to go to Mary Josefa's today. That is, her Russian friend's, Daria Ippolitovna's," she said, amending the lie. "And I imagine we shall see Vladilena Maximovna. After that, of course, I am sure we can avoid all polite society."

19

T hey were to be disappointed, however. Mary Josefa, it appeared, was unwell, so Daria Ippolitovna was not entertaining.

She had the goodness to tell them herself, though, and she came to the door covered in the sort of smock they had often seen Madame Chatel wear. It was a large white thing, flecked in paint.

"Well, I suppose we can see you another time," said Louisa-Margaretta, shifting on her feet, already prepared to leave. "Miss St Clair and I will have to seek out another source of amusement."

No doubt Louisa-Margaretta meant for them to traipse about the city, as she had the other day, perhaps freezing in the streets before they found anything that might point to a murderer. Judith desperately looked about for an excuse. Should she pretend to faint, that they might be allowed to rest there? Only such antics usually did not work quite so well with women, she had observed. The old story about feeling as if one might faint due to the cold was less likely to work with a populace inured to such weather, and she certainly could not afford to have them discover anything about Louisa-Margaretta's delicate condition.

"Are you painting today, then?" asked Judith quickly.

Daria Ippolitovna huffed. "Yes, as I'm sure you can see. Painting, with a friend. So that is why I have not been at home to callers."

"Well then," said Louisa-Margaretta, but Judith shook her head.

"You must come visit the Cluetts' home again! I did not see you at our little Christmas gathering, and you must have a chance to work with dear Madame Chatel." Judith had run out of things to say by then, but Louisa-Margaretta got the point and took up the mantle.

"Oh, of course," said Louisa-Margaretta. "She is the most brilliant painter I have ever seen, and I am sure she would love to paint with you. Of course, how many painters have I seen? It is not every day that I am given the privilege of staying with one of the most famous painters in Europe!"

Judith gave a smile, and it was sincere. "She is very kind. Very welcoming."

Daria Ippolitovna was nodding, so Louisa-Margaretta added to her praise. "Do you think your friend might wish to meet her? All would be welcome, of course. Madame Chatel loves to meet accomplished ladies."

The young Russian widow looked over her shoulder then invited them in. "You may as well see what my friend is painting. I am sure she would also love to paint with Madame Chatel if she would have us. Then again, I am sure she would hardly refuse. The nature of her position means that no doors are closed to us in this city."

Now curious, Louisa-Margaretta followed them. If Daria

Ippolitovna's friend was of even greater consequence, she must be wealthy indeed.

They entered a room where a familiar woman, upright and aloof, made practiced strokes on a large painting of a garden.

It was the emperor's youngest sister, Anna Pavlovna.

20

"Tell her." Louisa-Margaretta had been hissing this at Judith for minutes. But they could not contrive a way of ridding themselves of Daria Ippolitovna's firm and inquisitive presence. When they asked for refreshments, a servant was sent. When Judith was curious about the views from other parts of the apartment, she was invited to walk that way by herself while the other three ladies stayed together. When Louisa-Margaretta pretended that she wanted to see more of Daria Ippolitovna's paintings, she was permitted to take Judith and go see them. Finally, Louisa-Margaretta decided that they should leave, and she could whisper something to the princess as they were going. But instead, she noticed, with some horror, that Judith was lowering herself to her knees like some sort of religious figure.

"Please," Judith said. "I feel that we ought to pray, this very moment."

Louisa-Margaretta, when she was home, could always tell when her mother was about to pray. And she had perfected the skill of running out of the room before the prayer itself actually began. She was better than all of her brothers at escaping the many hours of prayer Mama would have them sit through and all the Bible reading and the fasting that would inevitably occur when they missed the first part of a meal.

Judith really ought to have warned her.

"Dearest heavenly father," Judith was intoning, "my friend and I are travelers in this land, but we are all travelers in spirit. Please, guide us in this winter of our hearts, let us know thy will, and make us instruments of thy peace."

She went on for many minutes, and Louisa-Margaretta could hardly keep from sighing. She ended up retreating from the room, as Daria Ippolitovna was also absorbed in the prayer.

It took her a moment to realize that Anna Pavlovna had also left the room and was now standing next to her, looking at one of Daria Ippolitovna's old paintings.

"She has gotten worse," the princess said, gazing at the portrait dispassionately. "She does not practice enough now that she has discovered religion."

Louisa-Margaretta nodded. "Well, perhaps when you visit, she will practice more. Your own painting is very well done."

Anna Pavlovna gave a courtly smile. "Yes, from a young age, I have been taught to paint pretty things. And if I am very fortunate, I shall paint more pretty things in my husband's house for the rest of my life."

"Are you to be married?" asked Louisa-Margaretta. It was not a delicate question, but she was so surprised that she did not stop herself.

"Soon enough," said Anna Pavlovna. "I may have escaped that Corsican devil, but I shall end up with someone else. I would not be at all surprised if my hand is auctioned off in Vienna. And I will be forced to leave my home forever."

Louisa-Margaretta, who had wanted nothing more than to leave her own home under the happy circumstances of a marriage to her dear Isaac, felt for Anna Pavlovna for a moment. Though Louisa-Margaretta's choice was greatly constrained, at least she had long been allowed the small dignity afforded to spinsters. Anna Pavlovna would never have such a thing. Princesses were never allowed to remain unmarried, not when a strategic alliance could bring such benefits to their better-placed brothers.

"Well," said Louisa-Margaretta. "Talking of Vienna, I shall speak plainly, because I don't think your friend Daria Ippolitovna would much enjoy hearing this. My friend and I are concerned that this lunatic who is going about town, harming your brothers, will come for you after this. And that he will finish by going to Vienna to kill your brother."

Anna Pavlovna laughed at this, and it transformed her face. All of the sour dignity melted away, and she looked how she had when she was absorbed in the act of painting. Like a child, which she almost was. Louisa-Margaretta remembered hearing that she was only nineteen and would turn twenty in January.

Poor Princess Anna Pavlovna. If she was thinking only of her impeding marriage and regarding it with dread, she was not likely to enjoy her birthday.

"Oh, they will not want to kill any of the ladies," she said. "Though if they ask where Catherine's bedchamber is, I fear I may tell them."

Louisa-Margaretta cleared her throat. She generally enjoyed jokes at her brothers' expense but found it rather shocking how much the princess despised her sister. "But how can you be certain?"

Anna Pavlovna shook her head. "It is one of the few compensations of being female. We are less likely to be killed, at least in this situation."

Louisa-Margaretta was saved from responding by Judith, who came in and clasped her arm in a show of feigned reproach.

"You ought to have prayed with us, my dear," she said. "It is restorative."

Louisa-Margaretta peered at her. She knew that Judith must have begun to say this in order to show off her piety for the religious Daria Ippolitovna. But it seemed that at least a part of her believed it.

"So it was," said Daria Ippolitovna. "And you ladies must stay and dine with us! We are very easy here, even when honored with the presence of the princess."

Louisa-Margaretta looked hopefully at Judith, who shook her head.

"We are going home," said Louisa-Margaretta without hiding her displeasure. "The Cluetts do not like us to be too much out of doors. We are to be sober and serious this whole season."

"Nonsense," said Daria Ippolitovna. "If you will not stay and dine, come mumming with us! Anna Mikhailovna is taking me with Mary Josefa tomorrow evening. We all know that the family rescued you from the cold, so the least you can do is help entertain them! At least one of her sisters will come, and as many friends as I can convince. Perhaps even our own Anna Pavlovna if she will be allowed out of the palace in costume."

Anna Pavlovna did not seem a very likely guest. "It's strange to go mumming in a city," she said. "It's a country custom! At any rate, you have not told me where you are going."

"Only to one or two houses," said Daria Ippolitovna seriously. "Chiefly to entertain invalids and people who are not getting to see the best of the festivities."

"Does Mary Josefa not disapprove?" asked Judith, incredulous, then Louisa-Margaretta saw her look down. Poor Judith! What must it be like to always wonder if one's curiosity is impertinent. Louisa-Margaretta never had to face such reservations.

Daria Ippolitovna blushed. "She does, a bit. Thought at first it would be too frivolous. But when I told her we were going to entertain people who might not get to go to a single party the whole season, she understood. She is a very good woman, a saint in her own right."

"I am sure she is not," said Anna Pavlovna haughtily, and Judith said, "I am sure she would not wish to be thought of as such."

"Oh, everyone wants to be thought saintly," said Louisa-Margaretta, taking Judith's arm so they might take their leave. "Especially those of us who least deserve it."

21

———

The next morning, Judith was most uncomfortable when they were seated in the sleigh. It was beautiful, and it had enough robes for all, but she did not quite feel easy around the Golenishcheva-Kutuzova family. After all, they were at the center of plenty of international intrigue, though they had the manner of simple girls, almost peasant-like. She was not fooled by it, though, and wondered what they were hiding beneath their air of unspoilt, childlike innocence.

And Mary Josefa, who was dressed as Saint Agnes, unnerved Judith. Putting one's hands in chains voluntarily, even as part of a costume, seemed many steps too far. Judith decided that this was what she disliked about mysticism generally. When she had begun to investigate the ways of the Quakers, she was drawn to their penchant for simplicity and silence rather than the showiness that she associated with the Catholic Church. At this point in her life, she was beginning to recognize that even her father's church had some rituals that she found unpleasant or overly gruesome. The Quakers were far less likely to worship images of Christ on the cross, for example, a change that Judith found more in keeping with her own spiritual preferences.

Daria Ippolitovna had designed her own costume, which appeared to be a large cloth with a great number of flowers. And Anna Pavlovna, dressed as she was by a number of skilled court seamstresses, had the best costume of all. She had come dressed as a bear, and she laughed every time she tried to make the proper sound.

Louisa-Margaretta, not to be outdone, had dressed as Queen Elizabeth I. The white makeup, which she usually put only on her hands, was now all over her face. Her hair was the perfect color, shot through with red and gold, and Judith thought she must have secretly relished dressing as a queen when there was an actual princess in their little party.

Not for the first time, Judith wondered why she had not contrived a way to go to Vienna, taking Louisa-Margaretta with her. Perhaps then, her friend could have married some penniless, insubstantial royal, thus gaining a foothold on the level of society where she had always believed she belonged. Weren't there scores of them attending, especially the ones from smaller countries that had been a part of the Holy Roman Empire, all hoping that some great power would give them a slice of their former glory? That was how the Cluetts put it, anyway.

Judith still longed for news, but she had to be careful of asking about it too often. The Cluetts did not like to predict which way the diplomatic wind would blow. The last time she had asked, Susannah Cluett had only sighed and reminded her that the thing was supposed to last for no more than a month or two in total. She had confided with her that it was very likely already finished. "I cannot imagine they would have gone past Christmas! But the post here is horrid; it will take us some time to hear the news."

A cold wind blew across the sleigh, and Judith shuddered. "Where are we headed, then?" she asked. Judith was dressed as a young boy with the beginnings of a mustache, and she felt rather uncomfortable wearing trousers. Her parents were always particular about her wearing respectable dress, so while she was used to corralling her brothers in her best muslin, she was not at all used to her current attire.

Marie Chatel was dressed as a Russian doll, a matryoshka. Her cheeks, already plump, looked quite beautiful with circles painted on them. Madame Chatel herself had done most of the makeup in addition to painting the canvas that Marie had made into a costume, so she looked exquisite. In fact, the preparations for their mumming brought together the longest stretch of harmony between mother and daughter that Judith had ever witnessed during her time with them.

"Only the most respectable homes, mind," Madame Chatel had harumphed as she added the finishing touches. "If you weren't going with a princess, you know I would never permit this foolishness."

"You used to go to plenty of costume parties, Maman," her daughter had said. "Many of them in very elaborate dress."

"None in an open sleigh in the middle of winter! What people will think on the street."

"There is nobody walking on the street. It is far too cold today."

"Well, exactly."

Judith was glad they had been able to bring Marie. It made the whole party seem less suspicious while giving them a chance to protect Anna Pavlovna from any would-be assassin. Judith was still not at all sure how to figure out who would be so radical as to go about murdering royals in order to change the fate of Europe.

She shuddered, saying a silent prayer for her fiancé, whose whole purpose in going to Vienna was to preserve some of the reforms and progress of Napoleon's era while washing them clean of bloodshed. Was his own mission so foolhardy as to prove absolutely hopeless? Louisa-Margaretta's brother had not thought so, and he had spent many years as a diplomat. One could only hope he was still watching over his cousin.

Judith knew she could not speak of it. But as soon as the thought crossed her mind, it began to torment her, and she had to say something. "Is there any news from Vienna?" she asked, gazing around the sleigh.

The other sleigh that had been next to them contained two Golenishcheva-Kutuzova daughters, Mademoiselle Chatel, and the young princess Anna Pavlovna. Perhaps it was fitting that the younger ones be there, whereas the spinsters and the widow were all together. Mary Josefa, Daria Ippolitovna, and some sort of lady-in-waiting shared Judith and Louisa-Margaretta's sleigh.

"What news might one expect?" said Mary Josefa rather cooly. "It is not holy, their gathering, and without the blessing of our divine judge, it will fail." She lowered her voice. "I would not say this before our younger companions, but the rumors that one hears from Vienna are rather shocking."

At this, the lady-in-waiting looked over all of them. "I must remind you that the emperor is currently in Vienna, as is his sister."

"Which sister?" asked Judith, worried. She had thought that the two sisters in St Petersburg, Anna and Catherine, were the only two who remained in the family. They had two elder sisters, both of whom had died. But she did vaguely recall another sister, married off to some minor European head of state. The very fate that Anna Pavlovna railed against for herself but would surely end up accepting in the end.

"Maria Pavlovna, Duchess of Saxe-Weimar," the lady-in-waiting said. "She is present at the conference with her husband. So I am sure we need not speak of salacious rumors, as there are certainly those present who are every bit as holy as one would hope."

Mary Josefa gave a smile, and if Judith had not known anything of that lady's beliefs, she would have sworn it was sincere. "Quite. I am sure you are right."

When they alighted at their first stop, Mary Josefa took Judith's arm. "My dear, you seem to have some questions about Vienna. What is it that you wish to know?"

Judith bit her lip as she followed the other mummers to the door. She had noticed that in the St Petersburg winter, it was customary to enter a home right away instead of standing outside for introductions. They were shown into a large entryway behind a grand set of doors, and the home was warm and inviting. But Judith felt very cold and not at all in the mood for dancing.

"Only how it is faring," she said to her companion as servants rushed off to summon the family. "Was it not supposed to have ended some time ago?"

Mary Josefa squinted at her, looking over both their shoulders to make sure that nobody else could hear. "It is a party of royal men, some of them with their stars rising, others made obsolete by these terrible wars. There are theatres and parties all about. Do you really think, under such circumstances, they will be eager to return to their families?"

Judith swallowed. She felt as if Morgan would know that she was disloyal if she did not immediately defend his character, though Mary Josefa's statements had been general.

"Some of them do not have families to return to," she said, hating herself for falling into a whisper. "Others are loyal, I am sure."

She did not sound sure, but it was the first part of her statement that seemed to interest Mary Josefa.

"Yes," she said. "Some of those men have nowhere to go. It seems rather English, or perhaps even rather Russian, to expect goodness and compliance from those who have lost everything."

Judith found the response surprisingly rude and realized that she had no idea what to say to it.

"I'm afraid I haven't the pleasure of understanding you," she said slowly. "Very Russian?"

But the expression on Mary Josefa's face had softened. "I must meet the family," she said as Daria Ippolitovna came towards them. Mary Josefa started towards the hosts, following quickly on Anna Pavlovna's heels, the chains of her manacles clanking together as she greeted everyone in her accented Russian.

Daria Ippolitovna gave Judith's hand a squeeze as they approached their hosts, who were taking their time exclaiming over every costume. "Don't mind Mary Josefa. She knows everything about God but almost nothing about Russians."

Judith must have looked shocked, for Daria Ippolitovna laughed. "It is a terrible thing to say, is it not? But true. You needn't worry about our royal family."

"But the pattern of these attacks," murmured Judith as their party was introduced to the hosts, a rather jolly family who seemed on very intimate terms with the princess. "I couldn't live with myself if it turned out some outside forces were responsible, trying to harm even such young people as Mikhail Pavlovich and Anna Pavlovna."

The group started singing, a Russian song that Judith did not know but soon began to get a sense of. She was always good with a tune, after all. And Louisa-Margaretta, who couldn't seem to muster enough Russian for any greeting, was singing the words beautifully after she heard the chorus only once. It told the story of a birch tree. Judith was surprised to find herself genuinely enjoying it.

After much applause, they were summoned to an interior room, where a very elderly lady on a fainting couch lay ready to receive them. *This must be the reason, then*, thought Judith. This lady looked as if she would hardly be able to bear even being carried from her front door to a carriage, yet her face grew bright and beautiful at the sight of the mummers. One of the Kutuzova girls went to sit next to her, and another did some kind of strange Russian dance as one of the young men of the home played a stringed instrument.

Judith wondered why the Kutuzova children should know such dances. They spoke French beautifully, even English, and had plainly received an education that was supposed to prepare them to move in the best circles. And yet this beautiful dance seemed like something that belonged to a peasant hearth, not the drawing rooms of a St Petersburg so enraptured with Europe that even Napoleon's reign had not been enough to stomp out its francophone tendencies.

Here, Judith drew closer to Daria Ippolitovna, by unspoken agreement, and the latter began speaking to her.

"Why would you suspect an outsider?" she said. "There are plenty here who are not happy with our government.

And you needn't look shocked. I know myself that such people exist, and I am not entirely devoid of sympathy."

Judith felt as though she were being tested. But she hardly knew what to say. If she expressed too much sympathy with rebellious tendencies, she risked being labeled a dangerous usurper. If she disagreed with Daria Ippolitovna, she would seem rude and ignorant.

She settled for a vague answer. "I can well understand why those who wish to protect their government," she said, her voice faltering, "might find it essential to pass reforms. Indeed, I feel much the same about England. If we are to keep our borders intact from one century to the next, we cannot ignore the changes within them. Even now, men who cannot work are suffering, and our government would rather mock them than pass the sort of reforms that would allow them to eat."

Daria Ippolitovna's eyes were sparkling. "You speak well, Miss St Clair. May I ask, are you political yourself?"

"Miss St Clair," said Mary Josefa, approaching at that moment, and Judith startled.

"Yes?"

"I hope you will join us for another song," Mary Josefa said, her voice throaty and beautiful. "As you can see, we are bringing a great deal of joy to our audience! And to spread such feelings, at this time, is holy."

Judith looked back towards Daria Ippolitovna, but the sparkle that had been in her eyes was gone. She was now wearing that expression of quiet reverence that so often came over her in Mary Josefa's presence. Judith found something about it unnerving. It was as if the vibrant young woman she had just seen had vanished entirely.

22

———

As they huddled in the sleigh, Louisa-Margaretta was thankful that the palace would be their final stop. They had already lost some time dropping that group of sisters in their home. There was some strange story about how they were not allowed to go to the palace, as their mother did not think it proper to appear before the sovereign's family in mumming costumes.

Perhaps Louisa-Margaretta should have made a similar excuse, as she was feeling exhausted. She had lost interest in each of their stops as soon as she learned that there were no eligible young men. She was worse than the girls she had come out with, really. At least they had gone mad over the handsome men, not just the eligible ones. She was like a scheming mama with an exceedingly plain daughter. The primary requirement was eligibility; all other things could be forgiven, even a rather dire lack of funds. And perhaps a plain, unassuming man would be better, as the competition for his favor would not be so heavy, particularly if he hadn't two kopecks to rub together.

Louisa-Margaretta wondered for a moment whether she

ought to learn Russian. Judith, who had been rather pale since their stop, was speaking rapid Russian with the lady-in-waiting. It sounded as if she were rather curious about the families of St Petersburg society. Most likely, she was just trying to be a matchmaker, and this irritated Louisa-Margaretta to no end. She hated the sensation of having to be rescued by Judith. Though she had enjoyed many privileges in society, the feeling of being an object of charity was a uniquely humiliating one. It was certainly a feeling that her mother must never have had. The way Mama went about in the village, swanning through with the choicest fruit for the poorest families, never stopping to think about how she might spare the recipients their blushes. How easily one's pride could suffer!

Louisa-Margaretta sighed, trying to think of the baby. For at the end of all this suffering, whatever her course, there would be a baby. At least then, she needn't dread the birth itself, for she would have a child.

The thought made her rather hungry. She had disliked being without an appetite, finding it an exceptionally unnatural state for her. She reached into the hamper that had come with the carriage, hoping that the palace had been able to supply them with something worth eating. Her costume was beginning to feel stiff and heavy, the white paint on her face doing nothing to shield her from the chill.

And, indeed, she was not disappointed. There was bread and meat and cheese, and if it was not perfectly arranged in the sort of sandwich she would have enjoyed, at least it was hearty. The dark Russian bread tasted rather strange to Louisa-Margaretta, and she wondered if the butter was clean. It seemed a bit grainy, and it had hardened in odd little clumps.

"Judith," she said, taking perverse delight in interrupting

her friend's conversation with her brusque sentences. "Do eat. You must be starving."

In anyone else, this would have been a courteous thing to say. But Judith was never starving. She never quite seemed to eat enough to meet her needs, and she probably recognized this statement for the bold lie that it was.

She was too polite to chastise her friend in front of other ladies and only said, "I will eat later. Perhaps just a small morsel now, if you have something ready."

Louisa-Margaretta could not help but grin. "Here, have some of the bread." She handed over a half-eaten slice with its grainy butter. She was glad to be rid of it.

"Would anyone else like something?" she remembered to ask, but the other two ladies demurred. Perhaps they knew that any food they might be given at the palace would be of superior quality.

By the time they reached it, which seemed to take an age, Louisa-Margaretta was feeling cold. Judith looked even paler, and Mary Josefa seemed stiff. Only the lady-in-waiting looked well, probably because she was coming to familiar territory. Not home, perhaps. Could one really ever be at home in a place like the Winter Palace, with its colorful grandeur and its strange mosaic of large, ornate rooms? Perhaps not. Louisa-Margaretta had enjoyed living in Wycliff Castle, but it was as different as the daughter of the house. As a royal servant, life would not be quite so simple.

Then again, it was during Louisa-Margaretta's time at Wycliff Castle that she had met the man who inspired her pitiable condition, and in a fit of madness and misery, she had given in to his furtive attempt at seduction. She still blushed to remember it, not because she was ashamed of the act itself but because she strongly felt that she ought to have done things differently. She could have waited for a grand passion, for someone who truly loved her and would lay down his life, not a sad man in a miserable marriage who had probably already forgotten her.

The memory was so shameful that she began to feel the pain everywhere in her body. It was in her stomach, her neck, her throat. As they arrived at the palace, all the ladies were helped down from the sleighs, but Louisa-Margaretta found herself putting her foot back up on the runner, trying to get into the blankets again.

"There, now," she said. "I'm afraid I need just another minute to rest. There's a good chap," she said in English, and the male servant who had been handing out the ladies looked at her blankly. Louisa-Margaretta, before darkness overtook her, had just enough time to see that Judith had been sick in the snow.

23

———

Judith never lost consciousness, though she saw Louisa-Margaretta faint. Afterwards, she wished that she could have done the same and missed everything that followed.

It was generally felt that the cold had been too much for the two English ladies, and a great coterie of palace servants was dispatched to bring them to a place where they might feel warm and comfortable. Judith, who had not the smallest intention of staying anywhere in the palace, tried to protest, but she found she was too weak. It took all of her concentration not to lose the contents of her stomach yet again, and so she did not object as much as she would have liked to, feeling at least thankful that she and Louisa-Margaretta were placed in the same bedchamber.

They were never alone, not for a moment, and the Russian girl who was specifically assigned to look after them was named Olya. She confessed this to Judith in their first quiet moment, when all of the people who had been fussing over them had left the room.

"You'll be well looked after here," she said. "They have cooks, doctors, all sorts."

"No doctors," snapped Judith, and she reproached herself when she saw Olya start at her tone. "I am sorry," she said. "But we do not need a doctor. If there is anyone we would see, it is Vladilena Maximovna. Is there any chance at all that she could be sent for?"

Olya was all good humor again. "People in this city are not in the habit of ignoring summonses from the palace, ma'am. Of course we may send for her."

After the only doctor that Judith could bear had been summoned, she had a chance to chat with Olya.

"There must be many children here," said Judith.

"Oh yes," said Olya. "They are all so delightful, the little things! Our dear ones are not blessed with living children, but we hope they will be before long."

There was a pause as they both considered this. Judith had known many families, including their own, who had lost infants and young children. That tragedy was universal, and for a moment, she thought of the Russian royal family as fully human.

"I also heard about a gentleman," she said. "A Mr Okhotnikov?"

Olya grew pale. "I am sure you are mistaken. No such person has ever been in residence at the palace."

Judith looked over at Louisa-Margaretta, who was breathing heavily on the bed. She had been in and out of consciousness, and Judith wondered whether she might be listening now.

"That is my mistake, then," said Judith. "I am sure I heard his name and simply mistook it for another gentleman's. These Russian names are very difficult for foreigners."

Olya's smile seemed a bit forced. "Of course."

"Where does he reside, this man?" said Judith. She had not wanted to bring up the name to anyone else, afraid of putting herself and her friend in danger. But now that they were already in peril, there was little sense in that approach.

"Nowhere," said Olya quietly.

Judith regarded her with skepticism. "He must live somewhere," she said gently.

"No," said Olya. "He is dead."

24

Louisa-Margaretta insisted on getting out of bed, and she told Judith as much. They had not been at the palace for an hour before she leaped up, going to the mirror to arrange her hair and costume. In spite of their troubles, she still looked like a creditable Queen Elizabeth, if a rather rumpled one.

"I'm not going to sit about like an invalid," she said. "There's a murderer here, and I'm not going to do nothing and wait for others to find him."

After a brief discussion, they had determined that it had not been the cold that had disturbed them. Though neither was a native of Derbyshire, they had lived there long enough not to fear a little snow. Rather, it must have been something that they had both eaten. Perhaps the butter, with its strangely coarse grains, was to blame.

"The murderer is probably not in the palace," Judith said. "Why attack members of the royal family only when they are not at home? Why not simply attack them here, when they are most likely to be unaware and vulnerable?"

"What a silly idea," said Louisa-Margaretta. "To draw

suspicion away from himself, our murderer can only act when he is away from the palace."

"There have not been a great number of people from the palace present at these parties," said Judith. "Perhaps the princes and princesses themselves, then another half dozen people?"

"Don't be silly," said Louisa-Margaretta crisply. "When you went to inquire about the carriage a few minutes ago, I asked Anna Pavlovna if I could take tea in her quarters. I'm going to learn more about all this, but you are welcome to sit and sulk if you choose."

"I think we should stop looking," Judith said firmly. "If whoever it is wants to kill the whole royal family, and perhaps anyone who gets in his way is in danger, we should get the Cluetts to make this public. And then we should escape."

Louisa-Margaretta only laughed. "Escape! Judith, we have dealt with plenty of murderers. You are acting as if this one is more of a danger."

"Perhaps," said Judith. "This is no murderer, Louisa-Margaretta. We are dealing with an assassin."

"All the more reason to start as we mean to go on. Oh, honestly, Judith! You can't sit here like some old woman, waiting to be murdered in your bed. If all of Europe depends on us, we really ought to be learning more than we have."

Judith felt as if she could never leave her seat. She was so very tired. "I would rather live," she said. "Is that strange to admit?"

"Nothing will happen to us. We were in the same party as the princess, don't forget. I'm sure this assassin you refer to has no idea of our existence."

Judith could not be sure.

Louisa-Margaretta did not wait for a response. After perfecting the twist of her hair, she strode out the door. Judith touched her fingers to her own thin hair, closing her eyes. She had not wished to wear a turban ever again after the events of the Christmas gathering, and so she had resorted to one of two rather dull caps that she had brought with her.

The spires of the cathedrals, strong outside her window, were dusted with snow, and they made her long for safe passage back to the Cluetts'. At least there, they could be certain of a welcome, and the passages were not crawling with strangers.

There was a knock at the door.

"I had to come see you," a voice boomed. "The rumor is that our Russian winter has laid your friend up again."

Judith averted her eyes. She judged it best to maintain the lie she and Louisa-Margaretta had agreed upon. Though someone had made a clumsy attempt at poisoning Anna Pavlovna, the two English ladies had decided to say nothing at present. Let the would-be murderer think their efforts had gone unnoticed, and perhaps it would be easier to catch them out.

"Your Russian winter is very harsh indeed, Monsieur Zharkov," said Judith, standing briefly and allowing the young man to kiss her hand. Blushing, she sank back down into her chair.

"Tell me," she said brightly, "what exactly would be required if my friend and I wished to winter somewhere warmer? St Petersburg is lovely, but perhaps Moscow would do better for the winter. Or even south of there if we could manage it."

The young man settled himself rather too near her, and Judith could see him thinking carefully about her question.

"It is largely a matter of luck and expense," he said. "There are plenty of places to change horses, of course, but the road can run from passable to dreadful. Or you might get some versts away from the city then discover yourself stranded between here and there. And, begging your pardon, many of the stopping-off places are not suitable for a lady."

Judith thought it best not to enlighten him on the nature of some of the places she had stayed, even lived. Though respectable enough, she was used to rather rougher living than he probably imagined.

"So you do not think it wise, then," she said quietly. "Even if we were willing to go very slowly and stop when we must?"

"Not at all. And the way that your friend wilts in the snow, like a flower! Many of our women are also delicate, but not quite so much as that young lady."

Judith sighed. "No, I suppose not."

"Do not despair," he said. "You shall both make it through all right, I assure you!"

"I am sure we shall."

The young man was not the wisest, but his brow crinkled. "You do not believe me."

Judith rubbed her head. "I am sorry, but I feel rather ill, even now. Would you mind seeing if the doctor has arrived?"

He was solicitous and kind, rushing off as soon as she asked it. And Judith had only to feel ashamed, for though she could not be honest with Monsieur Zharkov, neither had she found it within herself to tell him of her understanding with Morgan.

Each day, this omission weighed heavier on her, and she now had the feeling that it was too late to begin.

25

"I came as soon as they sent for me," said Vladilena Maximovna, setting her large bag on the floor next to her. "The message was that you were unwell due to the cold. But they took me to your friend first, who has not allowed me near her."

Louisa-Margaretta, who had followed the doctor through the door, glared at her. "It's Judith you ought to look at," she said.

"Louisa-Margaretta, you were the one who fainted," Judith said. "I'm sorry, Doctor. She seemed willing enough to let you examine her earlier, but—"

"Oh, I need no examination," said Louisa-Margaretta. "Only these ladies have been very naughty, giving me sweets and wine. God, how I would love to live in a palace!"

Judith pursed her lips at the blasphemy. If Louisa-Margaretta was drunk, she would have found out nothing about the assassin. Worse, she might have put their lives in danger by revealing things.

"Perhaps you will take a stroll with me, Judith," said Vladilena Maximovna. "You should be on your feet and moving. It will do you good. I shall do the same for your friend when we return."

Judith was puzzled, for she had not gone ten paces out of the room before the doctor placed a hand on Judith's back and leaned towards her, whispering as if they were sharing girlish confidences.

What she said, however, had very little to do with infatuation or fashion.

"Put furniture in front of your door," she said so softly that Judith could hardly hear. "Lock it, but drag something there so it cannot be easily opened. And do not stay in your rooms alone. Especially not with a man."

Judith, ever sensitive to appearances, frowned. "I thank you," she said without whispering. "What exactly are you implying?"

She was too angry to pretend that she was not offended. She felt it particularly because Monsieur Zharkov was always contriving to be alone with her. It was certainly not the other way around!

"You are clever, Miss St Clair, but there are many things you do not know." The doctor had also ceased to whisper now that her words could have been interpreted any number of ways.

Judith was fast growing impatient with being told that she was an outsider. She could not think of anything so obvious. "I would be obliged if you would provide me with an example," she said, trying to hide her discomfort by walking.

But Vladilena Maximova stopped her again, putting her large bag in front of Judith. "What a shame that the Golenishcheva-Kutuzova girls could not join you here at the palace. Did they give a reason, I wonder?"

"Their mother did not think it proper," said Judith.

"Something about wearing mumming costumes in the presence of the sovereign's family."

The doctor frowned. "Yes, that could certainly be a problem. Depending on the costumes, of course. Then again,
those girls never really come to the palace, do they? They
are in favor with the best set, of course, but one only ever
sees them in other places. Never here."

"Are you a frequent guest at the palace?"

She pursed her lips. "If you are trying to make me say
more, my friend, it won't work. And no—I am an infrequent
visitor, but my brother is often here."

"And his wife?"

The doctor's expression changed. "Rarely. She has
devoted herself to the set that believes that a woman ought
to be in her home at all times, making it pretty and perfect."

Judith did not miss the sarcasm in the woman's voice.
She had, however, noticed that the very rich did seem to
have beliefs about women staying in their own homes,
though clearly, trips to the seaside and the country did not
count against this. Nor did social occasions, such as visiting
with friends. Or shopping, of course, or the opera. Judith's
mother had often been home, but that was more to rest in
between her duties as a vicar's wife and the many hours she
spent helping others. If she had been a wealthier woman,
she most likely would have found many ways to amuse
herself in society while still insisting that a devoted wife and
mother ought to be home frequently.

"Your sister-in-law wanted a portrait," said Judith
thoughtfully. "She tried to commission one, but Madame
Chatel is rather busy."

The doctor scoffed. "Yes, unlike my brother's wife, she
must earn her living."

Judith nodded. "It is a gift to have a talent such as hers, though of course she has spent many years nurturing it."

The doctor, who had finished gathering her things, nodded in farewell. "I won't keep you, Miss St Clair. But I trust that you will neither repeat nor ignore what I have told you. See that your friend is not foolish either. In fact, if you find that her illness is such as requires a person at her bedside, you may wish to fulfill that duty yourself."

After Vladilena Maximovna left, Judith found herself growing sick with worry. She decided to find Louisa-Margaretta and insist that they be returned to the Cluetts', with the excuse that it would be more restful. She did not much like the idea of barricading herself in a room using heavy furniture, and she would feel easier if she were close to Madame Chatel. Though the painter had hardly been in fine spirits, she had an instinct for danger, and Judith was beginning to see how much they would come to rely on it.

26

Louisa-Margaretta had hardly been back at the Cluetts' home for a moment when Judith began going on about the Kuzmin family.

"I feel that they could be the key to the whole thing," Judith said. "Vladilena Maximovna told me that her brother is frequently to be found visiting at the palace. And he would have been able to put something in the baskets if he had wished to. She said some strange things to me, and I think she may have been warning me that he was dangerous."

Louisa-Margaretta's appetite had returned in full force. She could not stand to spend her days eating little, so she was having what turned out to be a rather delicious Russian pastry. Louisa-Margaretta refused to stay in bed, so they had the sitting room to themselves. Madame Chatel and her daughter had gone with the Cluetts on a visit. Though she and Louisa-Margaretta were quite alone, Judith kept looking about, murmuring.

"I don't know what troubles you, Judith." Louisa-

Margaretta took another bite. "I hardly think that the poisoner is in this household."

Judith regarded her wryly. "Clearly not."

"Would you have me starve?" said Louisa-Margaretta, savoring the delicious meat and cabbage inside the pastry. She took another mouthful of tea. Even in the ambassador's home, the tea was not what she would have wished, but with enough milk and sugar, it was tolerable.

"I doubt I will ever see you go hungry," said Judith.

But her words caused Louisa-Margaretta a bit of unease. Would her own parents wish for her to starve? Certainly not, and yet they might give her very little money if they were to discover the truth. Her head began to hurt once again. The daily physical reminders of her condition were becoming detrimental to her spirit, and she recalled once more what her quest had once been. She was going to find a husband then return to England with a man and a baby. And a nurse for the baby, of course. Louisa-Margaretta herself had never much liked infants and their messes. Better yet, they might go live in some European capital for a year or two, just to get the dates rather hazy in everyone's memory before they settled in England.

In fact, Louisa-Margaretta was not sure whether she would even wish to return to England if she were married. She had never gotten to do the sort of Grand Tour that all of the young men in her circles bragged about, and with a husband, she would be allowed the joy of discovering many continents that had hitherto been forbidden.

He would have to be the right sort of husband, of course. Someone her parents would approve of, either a rich man or someone who would make Mama and Papa eager to part with a rather large fortune.

Best that he be someone intimately connected with the

palace, then. Whatever Judith thought of the doctor's brother and his wife, they were certainly in one of the first families, welcome in every drawing room and palace in St Petersburg. Perhaps there were a few bachelor men in the mix, from their wealthy relations or something comparable, who would see only Louisa-Margaretta's beauty and overlook any swelling under her skirts.

"Very well," she said, taking a handkerchief and making a rather unladylike swipe at the crumbs around her lips. "I agree that we should become intimate with the Kuzmin family. But why would they wish to see us? I believe Mrs Cluett said that she is not close with Mrs Kuzmina."

"That is true," said Judith. "But Mrs Kuzmina would very much like to have her family's portrait painted by the finest exiled portraitist that money can buy."

The painter herself came in at that moment, ready for tea. She had divested herself of her cloak and muff, but her cheeks remained pink from her brief foray into the cold air.

"Money cannot *buy* me," she said haughtily in French, though she had clearly understood their conversation perfectly. "I paint where I wish, and I certainly find Mrs Kuzmina most disagreeable. To be confined in a cold room for hours with such a woman? Pah! My fortunes have not fallen so low."

"Yes, but you could name a much higher price," said Louisa-Margaretta. "Mrs Kuzmina wants what the finest people in this city want, and she is the sort who will even boast about how she had to pay more."

Judith nodded. "Indeed, she will pay almost anything."

Madame Chatel gave both ladies a rather pointed look, and Louisa-Margaretta stared back. She had no idea what the lady was getting at, but she was not surprised when Judith understood right away.

"Of course," said Judith hastily. "Let me be mother."

The Frenchwoman gave a rather throaty laugh. "I do not understand why you English ladies always say this. As if it were the only job of a mother, to be the person who pours the tea!"

Judith handed her a cup. Madame Chatel liked the Russian tea with sugar and no milk, which seemed a rather queer preference, but Louisa-Margaretta was thankful that Judith had remembered it. She would have put milk in instinctively, her desire to dim the flavor of the inferior brew overtaking any particular thought of Madame Chatel's preferences.

"I might remind you young ladies to offer me refreshments," said Madame Chatel. "It appears you have eaten all the food."

"Of course. I am so very sorry," said Judith, though she had eaten almost nothing.

"If I were you, I might avoid the food in this household. Or in this city, rather," said Louisa-Margaretta.

"One must eat," said Madame Chatel. "I daresay I have eaten worse. Do not forget, I was not born with a silver spoon in my mouth."

"True," said Louisa-Margaretta. "But this food may be dangerous."

"My dear," said Judith, but Louisa-Margaretta ignored her friend.

"Dangerous?" said Madame Chatel.

"Someone is trying to poison us," said Louisa-Margaretta merrily.

Madame Chatel spit out her tea then thrust the cup back at Judith. "Why would you tell me that after giving me the tea?"

Judith hastened to reassure her. "The tea is not

poisoned. We have both been drinking it all morning."

Madame Chatel's eyes were narrow. "The blackguards. It is just as it was in France! They will not stop with killing every member of the royal family. They will pick off all people of education and breeding one by one."

Judith opened her mouth then closed it. Louisa-Margaretta sighed, knowing that Judith had many inconvenient revolutionary sentiments. They had done little to endear her to Madame Chatel, who openly disliked Cousin Morgan for the same reason. Judith, of course, did not like to hear anyone speak about her fiancé, though Louisa-Margaretta thought her friend might now be willing to accept anything. Perhaps it was better to criticize Cousin Morgan and his silly ideals rather than remain silent on that subject.

Judith kept pretending that all was well, but the fact that no letter had reached them had become truly disturbing to her. Louisa-Margaretta had noticed, though she was far from worried. She could rarely be bothered to write, and even when she and Isaac had once maintained a frequent and passionate correspondence, she had only written half the number of letters that he did. She did not find it surprising that Cousin Morgan, while dashing about Vienna on his little diplomatic errands, had little time for letters.

"I tell you, Madame, we've been drinking the tea," Louisa-Margaretta said, grabbing the pot and helping herself to more. "So unless the poison is very slow to act, we are quite safe here. But none of us is safe when we go out."

She had been teasing, but Madame Chatel was sitting at attention now. "And you wish me to undertake this commission because you think that Madame Kuzmina's husband is a poisoner?"

"Perhaps," said Judith, who was always careful about slander.

"Yes," said Louisa-Margaretta. "And if he is not the poisoner, he likely knows who the culprit is."

"Why would he protect such a person?" asked Madame Chatel.

Louisa-Margaretta looked to Judith for an answer.

Judith, who was still daintily holding Madame Chatel's teacup, placed it on the table before adding just a bit of hot tea from the pot. One would not wish any tea, poisoned or not, to be served cold. "If we learn the reason, I suspect we shall discover the poisoner's identity rather easily," she mused.

Madame Chatel frowned. "And you think that this person will come after you again?"

"We do not know who his intended victim was," said Louisa-Margaretta. "It was probably one of the princesses, but now that we are looking into the murders, we may be the ones he wants to kill."

"None of us is safe," said Judith, though her tone was so very soothing that it seemed as if she were saying just the opposite.

"Very well," said Madame Chatel. "I shall undertake this portrait. But my daughter is never to darken the threshold of the Kuzmin home."

27

---

udith felt a chill as she crossed the threshold at the Kuzmin residence, but she dismissed it as silliness. After all, she told herself, she could ask for God's protection, not be bound by superstition.

And yet she knew one of her father's favorite parables about prayer. It was the one where the fool does not recognise all the different manifestations of God's aid and ends up dying from a rather foreseeable cause. After all, a loving God might very well put leaves in the wood that might be made into a poultice or a neighbor who can spare some of her eggs or a friend willing to sit up with a sick child. One might ask God for help, but the assistance itself might well come in the form of a human being.

And so Judith wondered if the foreboding she felt in the Kuzmin household was some sort of divine warning, one that ought to have her running out of the place. But thinking of the young princes and their sisters, she could not leave. If Kuzmin himself were evil, it was far better that she know it than that she leave others at his mercy.

The decorations were lavish. She was surprised to find that they were indeed rather tasteful, though Madame Kuzmina had spared no expense.

"Girls, you need not assist me in this sitting," said Madame Chatel as soon as their hostess had made a fuss of all of them. "I will continue when the children and Monsieur Kuzmin are present. For today, I shall begin with Madame Kuzmina."

"Monsieur Kuzmin may not be present for some time," their hostess said, arranging herself on an elegant sofa that rather overpowered the room. "I am afraid we may have to wait some weeks, dear Madame Chatel."

Judith met Louisa-Margaretta's eyes. This was not at all what they had anticipated! But it would be rude to inquire further, as there was just the hint of strain in the fluent French of the lady as she spoke.

"Wherever does he go?" asked Louisa-Margaretta. Worse, she continued. "I don't suppose he is spending all of his hours at the palace?"

Judith's smile was frozen on her face. She tried to think of a way to force Louisa-Margaretta to take back her intrusive questions, but no answer came to her.

"To be sure, I do not know," said Madame Kuzmina, who did not appear at all offended. "Sometimes, he is with friends or at the palace, and other times, he simply wishes to be away from home. He says that it is mine and simply the place where he sleeps!"

Judith had heard a similar joke from the lips of many women, and she had never found it funny. Indeed, nobody was laughing at this moment.

"Well," said Louisa-Margaretta, "perhaps you could send a servant to fetch him home."

"Pardon?" asked their hostess. Her smile was not quite so warm now.

Judith made frantic gestures, asking her friend to please not speak so, but Louisa-Margaretta's eyes flickered away from her. She was only pretending not to see, Judith was sure of it.

"Servants always know where a gentleman is to be found," said Louisa-Margaretta. "And it would be much easier for Madame Chatel to work if she had both of you present. Is that not the case, madame?"

The painter's eyes were shrewd. "Yes, to be sure."

Judith apologised. "She has a great deal of work this month, I am afraid. It may be because so many of the foreign guests in the city have a tradition of exchanging gifts at Christmas, as we do in England."

Madame Kuzmina brightened a bit. "Of course, dears. I should have thought of it."

After she had swept out of the room, either to summon a servant or to find someone who might escort them from the grand home, Judith began whispering to her friend.

"What on earth were you thinking? She will never have us back here if she hates us."

"We came with Madame Chatel," said Louisa-Margaretta languidly. "And what shall we learn from only this woman? Unless you think she may be the poisoner."

Judith frowned. Indeed, Madame Kuzmina had been present at each of the attempts on the royal family, apart from the poisoning of the food. But she would have had to be uncommonly clever to invent such a persona that even her sister-in-law would be entirely deceived. It seemed much more likely that she was exactly who she wished to be: one of the ladies very near the inner circle of the city's society but not quite in the first families.

They were prevented from speaking further by Madame Kuzmina herself, who came back in. "I have sent word," she said rather stiffly. "I am very sorry to inconvenience you, Madame Chatel. I am sure my husband will be with us shortly."

"Not at all," said the painter. "Please be easy. And you may feel free to converse in these early stages. I shall let you know when I am ready to put in the mouth and the eyes. Miss St Clair, perhaps you can position Madame Kuzmina so she is in the right light from the windows."

"Of course," said Judith, walking over to gently guide the lady to an appropriate position. A slightly plainer chair stood in a position where the light looked well on her delicate features.

"It is much better being painted by a woman," said Madame Kuzmina. "All of the artists who have come here before have been men, and I must confess it is rather odd having to sit in silence for hours."

Madame Chatel gave a sad smile. "So have many women felt, madame. Many women prefer another woman's presence, especially if they are surrounded with children."

Judith, who knew that Madame Chatel would be thinking of Marie Antoinette, hastened to speak of something rather more cheerful. "How elegant the young princesses are! I must say, it is a pleasure being in the society of so many kind and accomplished young ladies."

Madame Kuzmina gave her a curious look. "It is not very usual to speak of them in such terms, Miss St Clair. At least not here in Russia."

As Judith was apologizing, Louisa-Margaretta looked over. She had gone to the window, no doubt out of boredom, but something in the conversation had finally caught her curiosity.

"We are naturally respectful of our betters," said Louisa-Margaretta. "However, it is not unusual to be on rather intimate terms with members of the royal family. Indeed, if one has enough space, one may even entertain them as visitors."

Judith caught her breath and saw Madame Chatel hesitate over her palette just a moment too long. Both of them well remembered what had happened the last time there had been visitors of royal blood at Wycliff Castle. And, of course, even during an uneventful visit, it would never be the same as a real friendship. Those in line for the throne, even if they were rather low in the pecking order, would naturally expect a certain level of deference from even their most elegant hosts.

Madame Kuzmina, however, was warming to the subject. "It is this way with all the foreign visitors," she said. "One family from the Netherlands was very offended by our ways. There, I suppose, the king and queen are but half a rung higher than most of the aristocratic families. But here in Russia, it is not so. There is much about the family that we consider absolutely sacred. We would never speak ill of a member of the royal family, for example, no matter how intimate our acquaintance."

Judith saw Louisa-Margaretta listening with greater attention. Perhaps Madame Kuzmina was not quite as unobservant as she seemed.

A servant entered the room and said gruffly, "Monsieur Kuzmin and Monsieur Solier." Though the pronunciation was certainly Russian, they were all able to recognize the names.

Now, of course, further conversation on the subject would be impossible. Judith was relieved to see that whatever seriousness Monsieur Kuzmin brought with him, his companion was unlikely to be similarly burdened. The composer greeted Madame Chatel very warmly indeed and was courteous as he addressed the rest of the ladies.

"I thought you might require some music, so I brought a musician," he said. "Indeed, sitting for hours for a portrait must be very dull indeed."

"Not with such wonderful ladies present for conversation," said Madame Kuzmina, her eyes sparkling once more. She seemed to have forgotten that she had been deftly dancing around some of the topics that had been raised thus far.

"Indeed," said Louisa-Margaretta, meeting the eyes of the young man. "If there is music to be had, why should you suppose that you would be the one to provide it, Monsieur Solier?"

There was general laughter, though Judith did not join in. She hoped that Louisa-Margaretta would not get them thrown out. They were supposed to be learning about the family, not antagonizing everyone. Though Louisa-Margaretta was often witty, usually, she was more graceful with her barbs.

But she noticed that the composer was regarding her friend steadily.

"What would you propose, then?" Mr Solier asked.

"We shall both sing in Russian," said Louisa-Margaretta firmly. "Our hosts can decide whose music is better."

The composer frowned at her. "Well, then. Will you play?"

"My friend will," said Louisa-Margaretta. "Judith, please. To the pianoforte."

Judith found the instrument beautiful and the keys yielding, but she had no idea what she would play.

"Play 'For Oft on Wings of Evening,'" Louisa-Margaretta murmured to Judith. "Just once through, there's a good girl."

Judith tried to smile as she whispered to Louisa-Margaretta, "But that is one of ours, not Russian!"

"Trust me," said Louisa-Margaretta with a winsome grin.

And so Judith began to play one of the songs that they had written together. She realised that it had been quite some time since she had been able to sit at the pianoforte, and she was proud of the composition. But she wondered what would happen when her friend began to sing. Louisa-Margaretta's Russian seemed to have gotten rather worse since they'd arrived, and Judith could not imagine that she would manage more than a line. She had certainly never tried to get the words translated, and she knew that it would be too difficult for Louisa-Margaretta to figure out how to sing them on her own.

But Judith was surprised. As soon as she started to play the bars that required a singer, Louisa-Margaretta's lilting voice joined in. She sang with candour, with confidence, and it was some bars before Judith realised that her friend was singing absolute nonsense. Some of the sounds were Russian, to be sure, but the words did not mean anything. She tried not to smile, pursing her lips and pretending that she was reading the music that had been set in front of her instead of playing a song by heart.

The Kuzmins were also exchanging smiles at the false "Russian" words, but because Mr Solier was in front of them, he did not see. At the end of the piece, there was a good deal of applause, and Louisa-Margaretta made a little curtsy of acknowledgement.

"That was very well done," said the handsome young man, more alert than Judith had usually seen him. All of the boredom that seemed to enter his features on any social occasion had fled. "What an odd song! It sounds like Russian words and English music. Whoever wrote it?"

"A little arrangement based on an old folk song," said Louisa-Margaretta quickly. "Now, what do you have to sing?"

He blinked. "A great deal. Only I have not been able to write anything in Russian, as I do not speak that language."

"But you have learned some of the songs, surely," said Louisa-Margaretta, her surprise false but rather convincing. "You have not been living in this grand city without learning a single word of the language that is spoken here?"

"Well," he sputtered. "I suppose I have been relying on French. After all, Russian families, such as our hosts—"

"It is understandable," Judith said. "After all, Russian is a very difficult language."

She had been quite sincere, but Louisa-Margaretta only laughed. "All the more reason to study it carefully! Shall we say that I have won our little wager?"

"I do not recall any sum of money being mentioned," the young man said, now looking distinctly uncomfortable.

"You have certainly won," said the serious Monsieur Kuzmin, beginning to smile. "Well done, Miss Haddington."

"Thank you," said Louisa-Margaretta.

"Truly," said Mr Solier, chastened now. "It was lovely. Elegant but haunting. I must know the composer!"

"My friend, Miss St Clair," said Louisa-Margaretta.

He laughed at first, but he was the only one. When nobody else was amused, Mr Solier peered at Louisa-Margaretta.

"And the words as well?" he said.

Judith sighed. Surely now, Louisa-Margaretta would be forced to reveal all.

Her friend smiled. "Not Russian for anything. It was all

nonsense! Really, my dear Mr Solier, you ought to be ashamed of yourself."

"I?" he said.

"Yes," said Louisa-Margaretta. "I may speak very little Russian, but at least I might recognize the language were it sung right in front of me."

And the room rang with laughter.

28

Louisa-Margaretta stood by the pianoforte for a good deal of time as Mr Solier played his way through different pieces of music. She stated that she did not wish to hear anything of his unless it were written expressly for her, so he played none of his own compositions. But they found that they shared many favourites. He must have thought that he was simply passing a pleasant afternoon with a rather musical Englishwoman.

Louisa-Margaretta, however, had rather different ideas about the matter.

She made sure to drop as many markers of her family's wealth and status as possible into the conversation, mentioning that her family lived in Wycliff Castle many more times than was strictly necessary. She exaggerated her family's familiarity with the English royal family and spoke in loving terms of the occasion when she had been presented at court. In point of fact, that day had been rather awful, only tolerable because Louisa-Margaretta shared a carriage with a friend who was similarly ambivalent about the occasion. But she did not speak of this.

The next day, Louisa-Margaretta decided to ask for Judith's opinion on the composer, which was a rather serious matter. But first, they had to speak of their plans to find the murderer.

Louisa-Margaretta and Judith decided that based on one of Judith's conversations with the Kuzmin family, the Prussian ambassador was himself a likely murderer. He had made some strange political declarations about equality during his first weeks in St Petersburg, and though his remarks had been overshadowed by his excellent and careful politeness after the fact, they had not been forgotten.

And Louisa-Margaretta knew there were other reasons to suspect the man. After all, everything had begun under his roof, and he would have had plenty of opportunities to commit the other crimes. Judith pointed out that he was otherwise occupied when the youngest prince was pushed off the bridge, but Louisa-Margaretta was convinced that he could have had someone else do his bidding.

"They are even now divvying up all of Europe," said Louisa-Margaretta briskly. "Prussia will come out the winner only if Russia is distracted."

"So you would have me believe that they have somehow directed all of their ambassadors to harm royal families?" said Judith.

"There is a great deal of bizarre behavior in Vienna at the moment and plenty of corruption," said Louisa-Margaretta. "It is a dangerous time."

Judith only sat and stared, making no reply at all.

Louisa-Margaretta sighed. "There you go again. I am supposed to be the one who is glum, have you forgotten? As the only one of us who must marry immediately, my situation is the more pitiable."

"Do you really believe Vienna to be dangerous?" asked Judith.

"Only if you do not trust Cousin Morgan," said Louisa-Margaretta. "He is not a very imaginative sort, and I dislike his religion. But I can tell you this: He adores you just as much as you deserve. And though he is a great dullard, that fact alone makes me think well of him."

Judith was still silent.

"Judith," said Louisa-Margaretta. "Please consider. Even if there are mad Prussians going about, murdering foreigners, there is no reason to believe that my cousin will be on their list. He is English, he has no royal blood, and he has been a diplomat for all of two minutes. Nor is he likely to continue in this profession."

Judith started. "Whatever do you mean?"

"He is not an adventurous man, Judith. I am sorry to speak ill of my own family member, but it is the truth. He will want one little cottage where he can live forever, not this life the Cluetts have, posted to a new capital every month or so."

Judith only sat without answering, and Louisa-Margaretta could see tears forming at the corners of her eyes. She could not abide such sentimentality.

"For heaven's sake, get ahold of yourself, Judith," she said. "Sit here by the fire while I go speak with the mad Prussians."

"What are you going to say to them?"

"I shall think of that in the carriage," said Louisa-Margaretta. "It will come to me!"

This was all rather grand, of course. She had no real idea of what to say to the Prussians. And before she could leave the house, Mr Solier was shown in to see her.

"Monsieur!" she managed to say. "It is rather early."

Judith, giving a sly smile, withdrew with a curtsy. Louisa-Margaretta had not had a moment to speak to her friend about the interest she had sensed from Mr Solier the evening before.

It appeared that to Judith, this had been plain enough.

"I wished to speak with you," Mr Solier said. "It would be an honour to hear more about your life in England, your family there."

Louisa-Margaretta gave a polite smile, her mouth firmly closed. She had heard many people ask questions of this sort before! He wanted to know about her prospects.

"I am the youngest of many but the only daughter," she said. "My fortune is thirty-five thousand pounds. And my parents are eager only for me to make a respectable match, as I am old enough now that they have quite despaired of me."

"I cannot imagine anyone despairing of a young lady so elegant and beautiful as yourself, mademoiselle," said Mr Solier, lowering his voice.

Louisa-Margaretta only laughed. "It is no good. I am quite an old spinster. You had better find some pretty Russian girl with her own fortune."

He looked at the floor. "It is true, I am not earning the sort of living that some might wish for. But my devotion to my art is unwavering, and so must be my devotion to my wife. I cannot simply marry any woman, someone without the talent and taste to appreciate my compositions."

"Well, I know my taste is excellent, for I dislike many of your compositions," said Louisa-Margaretta. "Particularly that gloomy one you played for us yesterday."

"You see?" said Mr Solier, looking hopeful, and Louisa-Margaretta shook her head.

"You may as well leave," she said. "I am going out."

"Until tomorrow, then," he said, slowly taking his leave.

"Do you see yourself as a father?" Louisa-Margaretta said quickly. "That is, if someday you are to marry."

He gave her a look that nearly made her shudder. Unless Louisa-Margaretta was very much mistaken, he understood the exact nature of her question.

"I love children," he said firmly. "I have always loved them, all of the children I have encountered. And should I ever have the good fortune of marrying, yes, I would hope that the marriage might be blessed with children."

Louisa-Margaretta nodded stiffly. "Well, they have kept the carriage waiting. The horses will be cold."

He walked her outside and handed her into the carriage. She felt that she ought to be thankful for his answer, but the whole exchange had made her feel like weeping. Once, it would have been a pleasure to be courted by a handsome young intellectual. She knew that she was beautiful as well as rich, so even fortune hunters might not be lying if they claimed to be moved by her looks.

But for the first time, Louisa-Margaretta was in a position where she might have to beg for a husband. And she did not like this. Not at all.

She strode up to the ambassador's door with great impatience. It was time for her to demand answers. Perhaps she would not make a great marriage, but she had found murderers before. At least in this, she knew she could succeed.

29

Judith knew that Louisa-Margaretta had been trying to comfort her with all of those assurances that Morgan would not stray. The result, however, ended up being rather different. It brought all of the images back to her mind that she had endeavoured to forget. For even the Cluetts had heard the gossip about Vienna, how high living and wild affairs were just as much a part of the congress as its more official aims. And in Russian circles, tongues were always wagging over the widow of Prince Bagration in particular, who was apparently very alluring. And not short of money.

Shaking her head, Judith headed out of the Cluetts' home. She was going to take a walk to the Kazan Cathedral again, pray for her family, and forget all of this nonsense. If she could only find the faith that had deserted her! It was very hard, she noticed, to speak seriously of God when she was in the society of Louisa-Margaretta and her rich friends.

In some ways, it was no wonder that Louisa-Margaretta's mother had developed such a passion for religion. Mrs

Haddington was, perhaps, not always kind or subtle in expressing her devotion, but Judith never found her insincere. And Mrs Haddington had grown up in rarified circumstances, part of a family that had both wealth and an impeccable history. Judith, who was always intimidated by places such as Wycliff Castle, now realised that Mrs Haddington must have been surrounded by talk of balls, lace, and debauchery from a very young age. Louisa-Margaretta's mother wished for her own children to have a more meaningful upbringing, and she tried to force them all to share her faith. This had not exactly worked, but perhaps it was better than nothing.

Judith's breathing started to become more even as she approached the cathedral. It seemed to tower over the streets of Petersburg, and the sight of the Neva river also helped Judith lay some of her worries to rest. It might be frozen, but eventually, it would thaw, and she would go back to England.

She had been excited for this time in Russia, more than the stoic Madame Chatel or her wistful daughter, and certainly more so than Louisa-Margaretta, who was driven by silence and desperation. Judith, who did not have the means to travel widely, had been looking forward to learning Russian and immersing herself in the beauty of the frozen city.

But now, she looked at the silent buildings and saw only the danger that must be lurking inside them. She saw the beautiful snow on the rooftops and contemplated the dangers of icicles as well as the ease with which one could lose a finger in the dark winter. Even now, though it was late in the morning, the sun had hardly risen. What light it gave was masked by the clouds.

It was not easy to see in such light, and Judith found that

her eyes were seeking every detail of the street before her, as if the scent of danger were lingering on the wind.

When she reached the steps of the grand cathedral, she relaxed. Though her father had taught her quite firmly that God dwelled everywhere, from the humblest cottage to the meanest tavern, Judith still believed in her heart that churches had a sacred nature that ought not to be ignored.

But she should not have rested. Because as soon as she hesitated, a pair of strong arms slipped something over her head.

And then there was only darkness.

30

———

The Prussian ambassador's wife was full of smiles. She was ever so sorry that her husband was not in, and they were honoured to have such a guest as dear Miss Haddington! And the Cluetts had been ever so kind.

Louisa-Margaretta found that her smiles were empty. She was still hurt, humiliated, thinking about how poor Mr Solier had looked as he pressed his suit. How he had promised to overlook her past transgressions and raise her child as his own. Though she had once thought she wished for a man who felt those sentiments, now, they seemed abhorrent to her. For surely, he was only speaking that way since she had so clearly laid out what her fortune would be, down to the last farthing.

Louisa-Margaretta felt as if she were shrinking, and the beginning of one of her headaches began to plague her. To think she had dismissed sick headaches as an affectation, only because she had never suffered them before! And her head felt worse as she contemplated marriage with the troublesome Mr Solier. He was such a blatant mercenary!

Louisa-Margaretta had decided as a girl that she would not marry without romance, though her parents always exchanged looks of amused frustration when she told them this. Mama and Papa really should have been more sympathetic, as theirs was a marriage based on love and understanding, but they had not been quite so ambitious for their daughter. They seemed more settled on marrying her off to some innocuous cousin before she had a chance to enter into a scandalous elopement. The wrong marriage would see Louisa-Margaretta taken down a peg in polite society, and her parents did not trust her to choose wisely.

Though their efforts had been in vain, it seemed. Were Louisa-Margaretta to have a child out of wedlock, she would be a nobody in society, and things would be much worse for her than they might have been if she had married Isaac.

The thought still gave her a pang of remorse. As the ambassador's wife prattled on about the delicacies of the traditional Prussian new year's feast, Louisa-Margaretta allowed herself just one moment to think of Isaac. She had been getting along tolerably well without him, brittle but not bleeding, until a chance encounter in London had set her back. And ever since then, she had been unable to fully relinquish the idea of finding him again.

For the years since their engagement had taught her a hard lesson. She had seen men who were amiable, intelligent, and very handsome. But she had loved no man as well as she had once loved Isaac. Louisa-Margaretta had been forced to admit that she was not going to find a man who would replace him. The love they had shared would have to be a thing of the distant past if she did not keep herself a spinster, hoping that he would end his years a widower and ask for her hand again.

And even then, would his children wish him to marry me?

She knew the answer without giving the matter any thought at all.

The ambassador's wife was talking about marriage. It was an unavoidable subject, especially for a lady who was rather fetching and yet unmarried.

"I wanted to go to England and take the waters at Bath, as my eldest sister was living there," said the lady, her cheeks flushed. "Will you not have a glass of wine? I have developed quite a taste for it, I confess!"

Her statement was rather unnecessary. Louisa-Margaretta found that any ladies who drank wine before noon had rather too much of a taste for it, and she was repulsed. But then, she considered her own pitiable situation and decided that a glass of good wine might be just the thing.

"Yes," she said. "I will have some. Just a very little bit, of course."

"Oh, quite," said the young woman, but she had sent the servants away so she might gossip freely. She splashed some of the wine on the table as she filled Louisa-Margaretta's glass.

Louisa-Margaretta took a long sip. She had to, or she would have spilled it on her gown.

"At any rate," the young woman said, her cheeks even pinker now, "my husband said that he would not wait for me. Can you imagine it! Said that there were plenty of young women who would be happy to marry him in a matter of weeks, and he was not fond of a long engagement. The cheek!"

Then she blushed, perhaps realizing all of the things that a "long engagement" implied. Louisa-Margaretta was half tempted to tell the woman that she was no innocent, but she could not, of course. Respectable women were not ever supposed to be tempted into entanglements such as hers, but if they were, they should certainly never be so foolish as to speak of it.

"Could you tell me more about your husband's beliefs?" said Louisa-Margaretta. "His thoughts on the politics of the congress that is happening even now in Vienna, for example."

Her hostess burst out laughing. "Oh, you English ladies! All so very well-bred. But I will finish my story, of course. I thought that, if I were going to get him, I had better not go to Bath. And so we were married, and I have still never been there to take the waters. I most probably never shall now that my sister does not live there any longer."

In spite of herself, Louisa-Margaretta asked about the story. "Did you truly think that he would not have waited to marry, not even for a month or two?"

Her hostess looked solemn for a moment then took a deep drink from her glass. "I did not wish to depend on my family. Some money was settled on me, but I am not one of those fortunate women who had a great deal of wealth that was all her own."

Louisa-Margaretta nodded. She knew that such independent women were rare, even outside of England, and that the provisions made for the sons of the wealthiest families would always be central to the marriage market.

"So I suppose you married in haste," she said.

Her hostess smiled again, though Louisa-Margaretta wondered if her good cheer was feigned.

"Yes, I love my dear husband far too much to have allowed him to escape me," she said. "He does talk a great deal about politics, and I assure you, it is all very dull! You must tell me more of your life in England. I do so wish I could live in the countryside. And somebody told me that you both ride and hunt!"

The rest of the visit passed without any interesting events or information. Try as she might, Louisa-Margaretta could not learn any more about the ambassador, either his movements or the sort of beliefs that would turn him into a willing accomplice in a plot of international intrigue. Indeed, the more Louisa-Margaretta sat in the overheated sitting room, the less she believed that the Prussians were behind the attempts at murder. When she did listen to the Cluetts talk about the congress, what she understood was that the alliances were secretive and constantly shifting. How on earth would the Prussians be able to ensure that ridding themselves of some Russian royals would give them an advantage? Could it not lead to rather grave consequences instead?

She did, however, think a great deal about the young woman's confession of how she'd ended up marrying. Louisa-Margaretta thought that any man who would say that he refused to wait for such a bride must be a boorish sort. But she agreed, privately, that it was perhaps best to act quickly. A bird in the hand and all that.

And in her condition, perhaps she did not have the luxury of hesitation.

She left that outing to go back to the Cluetts', all the while thinking of how she might get things settled. If she were only married, she could figure out all the rest later on.

"We ought to go out in the carriage," she said to Mademoiselle Chatel, who had been sitting in the music room, plunking out scales with a lack of skill and a decided absence of discipline. "Let me tell Judith; she may accompany us. I thought we'd go call on the Dutch ambassador." She blushed a bit as she mentioned the family that was now playing host to her erstwhile suitor, Mr Solier, but Mademoiselle Chatel did not appear to notice.

"I have been looking for Judith," she said. "I wanted to speak to her about something I noted during our time at the palace. She went to the cathedral to pray. That large, ugly one not far from here."

Louisa-Margaretta rolled her eyes. "We need not expect her back for some time, then. Tell me what it is you noticed, but make haste. Perhaps you and your mother should accompany me."

"Oh, Mama is painting," said Mademoiselle Chatel. "Which is just as well. I don't wish for her to hear us." She lowered her voice. "I do not think that Prince Nicholas is behaving as a man ought to if he is in danger. Do you think that the attack on him might have been a false one?"

Louisa-Margaretta frowned. "It hardly seemed false to me. I do not see how he could have easily pretended to have such a brush with death."

"Yes," said Mademoiselle Chatel. "But they say at the palace that he often goes out unaccompanied, that he does not heed any reasonable precautions for his safety!"

"Well, he is young," said Louisa-Margaretta carelessly. She herself had always hated all the rules meant to protect her person and her reputation. She had only reluctantly agreed to have a companion when she was under the watchful eyes of London's gossips. In Derbyshire, she went out on horseback alone at all hours, and she refused to stay indoors even in bad weather. In fact, one of the reasons that she had been able to get herself into trouble in the first place was that her parents had despaired of controlling her movements. They might force her to retreat to a lonely mansion near a pitifully small village, but they could not keep her within its walls like some princess in a child's storybook.

And in the spring, she would be brought to bed. She shuddered at the thought, all the while wondering about the child. Would he or she take after the Haddingtons? She hoped so. It was hard even for her to remember the father's features, and she hoped the little one would have her red hair and her own father's brown eyes.

Mademoiselle Chatel lowered her voice. "If Prince Nicholas were afraid, as he ought to be, would he not take a little more care? After all, his father was—" She whispered the last part. "Well, he was killed."

Louisa-Margaretta had heard it already, of course. Though only in whispers such as this one. She had certainly heard the stories more often in England than she had since coming to St Petersburg.

The previous emperor, Paul, had not been well loved. In fact, it seemed he was not up to the task at all. As someone who had lived under the rather pathetic son of a powerful king, Louisa-Margaretta knew that brilliance often skipped a generation where monarchies were concerned. In fact, sometimes, it skipped several generations—or never reappeared at all.

"Very well," said Louisa-Margaretta. "I suppose we can ask someone about the prince's habits. But I do not know how we shall ever get invited to the palace again."

"There would have to be an occasion," said Mademoiselle Chatel. "Perhaps Mama will be asked to paint a portrait."

Louisa-Margaretta gave a dry laugh. "She is quite tired of painting portraits based on our little whims rather than her pocketbook. No, I shall think of something else."

The occasion, of course, would have to be her wedding.

Her stomach turned over at the thought. She tried to pretend, at least to herself, that it was the usual nerves that came along with such an occasion. But she could not.

Perhaps it had always been a lie, she mused. Older married ladies had many calm, humorous ways to tease the young ones when a wedding date approached. But Louisa-Margaretta knew that when marriages went poorly, things could be very grave indeed for the bride. Even in her spheres, whispers circulated about couples who "enjoyed their many homes," or "have, unfortunately, not been able to spend the Season together," and other such pretty phrases. And those ladies were the fortunate ones, as they had found at least some means of escape. If a young woman's family had no money or not enough affection to support her in her poverty, then all doors would slam shut on the occasion of her marriage.

What woman could marry in complete happiness, knowing of this possibility? Perhaps Louisa-Margaretta should not have been a spinster. Better to be young and silly then marry in haste, like the Prussian ambassador's wife. Louisa-Margaretta had never even learned the young woman's name, in part because it was unpronounceable and complicated, but also because the wine-loving young woman seemed so wholly defined by her station in life.

Louisa-Margaretta clenched her fists, glancing briefly down at her hands. They were not quite as white as before; she had neglected her cream for several days. She thought bitterly that she ought to take more care with her toilette, as without it, she might not be able to secure a husband.

Judith would know what to say. She was always a comfort when Louisa-Margaretta felt these pangs about her future, though she did tend to have sermons just as tedious as her father's about how Louisa-Margaretta ought to be thankful for her own privileges when so many people were starving.

I am thankful, Louisa-Margaretta thought. *I would simply also like to have married Isaac, lived somewhere besides this frozen Hades, and had some rather good hunting each year. Or at least one of those wishes.*

She looked at Marie Chatel. "You are quite right. Let us go and find Judith. I'm sure she is back by now and skulking about here somewhere, probably with a book. Then, we may all go out together."

31

Judith knew only darkness for a time. She was in a carriage, though, she was certain of that. The robe that was keeping her warm was of a fine fur, and she thought she could smell something familiar in the interior. There was a hint of summer, of the sort of perfume a lady would wear to a grand event.

Also, any carriage must belong to a wealthy person. When she asked where she was going, only one word was spoken to her, in French.

Silence.

She was not supposed to speak.

Judith had been used to looking after her own affairs from a young age. Even when her mother had been alive, as the eldest of all her siblings, she was often called upon to mind a child. And her father was always so busy with his parishioners that he relied on her help, not only her mother's. There were even times when both Judith's parents would have solemn conversations with the older members of a given household then ask Judith what the children had shared in unguarded moments. They knew that a very young child would tell another child whether the family had enough food or feared their father or had difficulties with a violent neighbor. Judith had always been taught that to solve one's own troubles was no small thing. When this failed, she was always told to ask God for help.

Judith prayed, of course. She ran through her favorite psalms, the words so familiar that she could pray without thinking. But she also had a strange impulse.

She expected Morgan to come to her aid.

Louisa-Margaretta was the more likely saviour, of course. She had burst into a room more than once just as Judith was about to get into very serious trouble, saving both their lives. She also had a gift with both horses and guns that many young men would envy. Morgan was quiet by nature, just like Judith, and as a Quaker, he did not believe in violence. It was one reason he had been reluctant to enlist in the army but eager to help keep the fragile peace of the European continent as a diplomat.

But Judith's soul called out to his, and she found herself believing that he would save her. For her love did not follow any sort of logic, and she was too scared to give up this small shard of hope.

The carriage came to a halt, and Judith was escorted out. She could tell that she was being taken not through a public entrance but through the door that the servants must have used. What a strange sensation it was! But the person leading her held her hand gently. They must not wish to harm her, at least not yet.

She found that she could not speak. Even so, when she was brought into a room with more people, she knew that she must.

"Please," she said. "I have no money. But I do have friends who would pay whatever they can. Please."

She was met with more silence.

32

Mademoiselle Chatel panicked when they did not find Judith in the house. Louisa-Margaretta's feelings were calmer, at least at first.

"She is probably still in that silly cathedral," she said. "Perhaps she will go the way of her father and decide to devote her life to God, meaning she will end up in a Russian monastery, wearing some silly costume. I shall have to learn at least a few phrases so I can make her leave! Judith is always enamored of new religions. Did I ever tell you about our time with the Quakers?"

But Mademoiselle Chatel would not be comforted. "I must tell Mama. She will know exactly what to do."

"You can't go running to your mama for every little trouble," snapped Louisa-Margaretta.

Mademoiselle Chatel's lip quivered. "But what are we to do, then? She can't have been in the cathedral for all these hours."

Louisa-Margaretta hated to think it, but the scared young woman was probably correct. Judith had been out for far too long, and it was most unlike her to worry her friends. She ought to have sent word.

So she and Marie Chatel went to the room where the painter was working. Madame Chatel only confirmed her fears. "You young ladies must learn to keep each other safe," she said sharply, putting down her paints and brush violently and tearing off her smock. Louisa-Margaretta, for the first time, was truly alarmed. Madame Chatel always took good care of her paints and brushes and scolded the young ladies when they did not pack them away to her specifications. If she would risk ruining them, she must be very concerned for Judith's safety.

Louisa-Margaretta frowned at her. "There is nothing to be done about that now. We must find Judith, and quickly."

"How?" said Mademoiselle Chatel. Her tears had now spilled over, and she took Louisa-Margaretta's hand.

Louisa-Margaretta would have shaken her off, but she noticed that Madame Chatel was exceedingly stern with her poor daughter.

"This is no time for tears," barked the painter. "Control yourself."

This only made the poor young woman cry harder, and Louisa-Margaretta stood between them, taking the girl's other hand in her own.

"Marie," she said. "Go along and send a servant. We must have someone check the cathedral. I do not believe Judith is still there, but perhaps she lost track of time during her prayers."

It would not be particularly like Judith to do so, but it was a possibility. Louisa-Margaretta's mother could pray for countless hours, with both social engagements and meals falling by the wayside all that time. It was one of many reasons that Louisa-Margaretta tried to escape whenever

Mama seemed to be in such a mood. The prayers were tedious and often felt unending.

Mademoiselle Chatel, with trembling hands, brought out a handkerchief. Louisa-Margaretta turned to the mother.

"Madame Chatel," she said. "You are friends with the Prussian ambassador and his wife. You must go see them and see if they have any idea where Judith might be. Then go ask the Kuzmins."

Madame Chatel would not go quietly. "You told me they could be dangerous. And yet you send me into the lion's den alone?"

"Take someone if you will," said Louisa-Margaretta. "Take Mrs Cluett. It matters not. Only go."

Madame Chatel did not outright refuse, and Louisa-Margaretta knew to take this as a compliment, though the painter's expression was sour.

"And you?"

"I will find the person who helped us before," said Louisa-Margaretta. "Monsieur Zharkov has shown me that he can find any lost person in this whole city. If he manages it this time, I will consider it a rather stunning proof of his abilities."

There was confidence in Louisa-Margaretta's voice that she did not feel in her heart. Trying not to think of what might have happened if they had eaten more poisoned food during the mumming or it they had been placed slightly differently during the attempts on Nicholas's and his brother's lives, Louisa-Margaretta called for her cloak.

33

Judith's appeal was met with silence for what seemed like ages. But finally, one person spoke to her.

"Dear Miss Saint Clair," the voice said. "Please do not mistake us. We did not bring you here for any nefarious purpose. Rather, your presence at our gathering is due to the trust we place in you and in your judgement."

Judith started. "Vladilena Maximovna. What are you doing in this place?"

There were titters and many voices speaking in Russian. Judith caught some words, but she could not understand what they were speaking of.

"I believe I know you best," Judith heard the doctor say. "And if I am not mistaken, you have many doubts about Russia's governance. Have you not been asking about Vienna rather constantly, perhaps hoping any developments may lead to great changes in St Petersburg?"

"I am hoping for news of the congress because my fiancé is there," Judith said. "This is no great secret."

"And Monsieur Zharkov?" said someone else.

Judith hoped that not enough of her skin was visible to

show any blush. "A friend. I do not even know him well! I am engaged to Mr Morgan Ramsbury, who is posted with a diplomatic delegation in Vienna."

"It is not a false front?" said a voice that Judith did not recognise. "Your interest in this meaningful event is truly *only* a romantic one?"

The disapproval was undisguised, and Judith opened her eyes behind the blindfold. It was strange not being able to address any of these ladies properly. She had a sense of the woman who had spoken, though. The voice was aristocratic and young, seemingly younger than most of the assembled company.

"We both have a great interest in the events," Judith managed to say. "They could change Europe forever. But I am concerned for Mr Ramsbury's safety. Surely, that is not strange, given the dangers I have seen here?"

There was some shifting.

"And what of the danger that all Russia faces if we continue on this course?" said a different voice. "With the royal family itself allowed to be ruler, judge, and executioner?"

"Goodness, I hope that nobody will be executed," said Judith in a clumsy attempt at levity.

No one laughed.

"Emperor Alexander murdered his father, and when his brother wanted—" said a voice, but they were interrupted by murmurings, and the speaker did not finish.

"Murdered his father!" cried Judith. "Surely, that cannot be true."

There was a long silence, then someone again ventured to speak.

"He was raised with the idea that he would rule Russia," another person said, and Judith recognised Vladilena Maximovna's voice once again. "His grandmother promised him the throne. When he saw the terrible mess his father had made, he agreed to the plot. He cannot have thought that the conspirators would simply let the old man live out his years in peace."

Judith was breathing quickly now. "But is that not an argument in favor of the current arrangement? Alexander is much more competent, surely? And he was quite a hero against Napoleon."

This time, she heard a new voice. This person sounded like an elderly woman, and the other voices were quiet in deference.

"Our Russian winter defeated Napoleon Bonaparte," this woman said. "What do we owe our emperor, he who lost our sons and brothers at Borodino? Our grandsons? He would listen to nobody. Deaf in one ear, and he chooses to be deaf in the other. Worse than I am."

"I am very sorry," said Judith. "But I fear I cannot join your cause. I am here as a civilian, truly. I am not even a diplomat myself."

"Most disappointing," said Vladilena Maximovna. "I had expected more of you, Miss St Clair."

Judith held her breath. She had not seen any of the women, but in her experience, people with secrets did not like to see them shared.

34

The carriage stopped very near the Cluetts'. When Judith arrived, only the ambassador was there to greet her. He offered her tea, and she accepted gratefully. Tea, such an ordinary thing! She had not eaten since breakfast.

"I am afraid the rest of the party have been out looking for you, Miss St Clair," he said as they sat down. It was the nearest to a reprimand she had heard from him.

"I am terribly sorry. I was asked to come take tea with a friend, and I quite forgot the hour."

He said nothing about her excuse and did not even look curious at her obvious hunger. She fell upon the light sandwiches that a servant brought them with great haste and only with difficulty restrained herself from eating with the rude abandon so characteristic of her friend Louisa-Margaretta.

"Miss St Clair," he said. "I will confess, something of your reputation had reached our ears before you came here."

Judith knew that Louisa-Margaretta had a reputation,

the sort that people whispered of in company. Though her parents had whisked her away to Derbyshire to ensure that no actual scandal came of her engagement with Isaac, the intervening years had not been kind. Louisa-Margaretta was considered rather flighty by all the cream of London society, though she had not yet done enough damage to her name to risk having to marry beneath her. There were still enough fortune hunters from good families that she need not look to the lower sort of mercenary. Though perhaps that would be different now.

All Judith could think of were the assumptions the secret society ladies had made about Monsieur Zharkov, so she could not answer the question implied in what Mr Cluett said to her.

He continued. "Yes, you and your friend Louisa-Margaretta have found yourselves in some rather unusual situations. But I was persuaded that you always assisted the cause of justice, or so the young Mr Haddington told me."

Judith swallowed. She hoped that the Cluetts' connection with Louisa-Margaretta's elder brother was not a terribly intimate one. It had been strong enough for them to take on three young ladies and a haughty painter when they hardly had room for such a crowd. Still, she ventured to hope that they were not going to be in very close contact with any of the Haddingtons. If they were, Louisa-Margaretta's secret would become known.

"I have been near death, sir," she said. "As a clergyman's daughter, I could hardly avoid this. But in the cases when my friend and I were forced to make inquiries, I hope we have been respectful in every instance."

The look he gave her was penetrating. She had been used to thinking of Mr Cluett as a silly man, fussy about appearances and little else, but she was certain that he did not believe her.

"We must all of us take very great care," he said. "There is a great deal about Russia that you do not understand, Miss St Clair, although you have grasped more of the language than the rest of us."

Judith thought it ought to be a scandal that Mr Cluett was content to speak in only French to all the people they encountered and wondered why he did not apply himself to his studies. But she was wise enough to stay silent on this point.

"I cannot disagree," she said. "But I am afraid that, with inaction, we would risk greater danger."

"That is where you are wrong," said Mr Cluett, his voice rising. "There are forces and rivalries at play in the palace that we ought to leave there. Our involvement would be not only dangerous but futile."

"So you believe the palace is at the heart of this?"

He shook his head. "I do not plan to speak of it. And neither should you. Your aim, in these months, should be to live a life above reproach here in the city. When the ice has melted, Madame Chatel has already expressed a wish to return to England, and it would be wise for you and your friend to follow."

Judith swallowed. She could not tell him of her plan to find a smaller city with Louisa-Margaretta, one where the child could be born in secret. This was only ever a last resort, and with any luck, they would not need it. She knew that her friend hoped to marry.

And so, pushing these thoughts aside, she squared her shoulders. "I am happy to leave it for today," she said, pretending to go along with his scheme. "But there is one question you might answer for me."

"Perhaps," he said guardedly, ever the diplomat. "If I have the answer."

"I heard—" Judith tried and failed to think of a way to describe the secret society. She cleared her throat. "Somebody implied to me that the emperor may have killed his father."

Mr Cluett looked around sharply. He rose from the sofa where he had been sitting and came to sit in a chair directly across from Judith. Even that did not seem to be close enough, as he dragged the chair so it was directly next to hers and leaned in. A person who did not see the expressions on their faces might have mistaken them for lovers.

"That sort of thinking," he whispered, "could put us all in very great danger."

"But could you tell me?"

He shook his head. "Forget you heard that rumor. And do not force me to spell out how dangerous it would be for you to ever repeat it again." He sank back in his chair forcefully. "Ah, I believe I hear the carriage," he said, more loudly now. "It will be some of the party. How silly they were when they lost track of you! These things happen, said I, but they would not listen."

Judith could not have said for whose benefit this was. She doubted any of the servants spoke enough English to understand. But when Louisa-Margaretta came in with Monsieur Zharkov, she was thankful for the diversion.

35

———

"You drove us all to distraction," said Louisa-Margaretta, scolding Judith. "We looked everywhere for you! And we only came back here because Monsieur Zharkov insisted."

The officer gave a sweeping bow. "Here is your friend, quite safe, just as expected," he said. "Did I not tell you from the very beginning that we would find her here?"

Louisa-Margaretta scowled. "You did tell me, then you were very happy to go all about the city looking for her. My fingers shall remain frozen for a century."

"Well," said Monsieur Zharkov, "how jolly that we are all here!"

He paused, apparently expecting some sort of invitation. Louisa-Margaretta was not going to give the man a thimble of gruel, much less invite him to stay for tea, but she saw that Judith felt their rudeness.

Mr Cluett, of course, made an offer of his own.

"I have some excellent port, Monsieur Zharkov," he said. "I wonder if you would share a glass with me?"

"Of course," said the man. "Ladies, do you enjoy drinking this English port?"

"I must dress for dinner," snapped Louisa-Margaretta, though they were not very near the time. "And I shall require Miss St Clair's assistance."

"Of course," said Monsieur Zharkov, looking downcast.

Louisa-Margaretta decided that he was too stupid to understand that she did not need to change before dinner, so she took Judith's hand. "Come with me, please," she said. "Do have a marvelous evening, Monsieur Zharkov."

As soon as they were upstairs, Judith began whispering. "Louisa-Margaretta. You can never imagine where I was taken!"

"Well, I thought you were taken by Monsieur Zharkov," said Louisa-Margaretta. "He is a very strange man. I thought he must have hit you over the head and taken you off to some remote country. Siam, perhaps."

Judith entered the room that she shared with Louisa-Margaretta first and closed the door. One could always tell when Judith was angry. Instead of slamming doors, like Louisa-Margaretta did, she closed them with the quietest little click. When she turned back to her friend, Louisa-Margaretta could see that her mouth was in a firm line.

"There is nothing wrong with Monsieur Zharkov," she said. "Though why everyone seems to connect my name with his, I could not say."

This was too much for Louisa-Margaretta, who began laughing. "He adores you, Judith. Though I do not trust the man, nobody could fail to see it."

Judith was frowning. "But he loves war. He wants nothing but adventure in life!"

"Perhaps he wants a little wife to keep his home tidy for him while he goes off to strange lands," said Louisa-

Margaretta calmly. "He is probably fascinated by someone whose character is so different from his own."

Judith was sitting on the bed now, clutching at one of the blankets. "Oh, I cannot have given him any notions! I have spoken often of your cousin, Louisa-Margaretta, you know I have. Our engagement is no secret."

Louisa-Margaretta smiled grimly. "Yes, well, a man like Monsieur Zharkov must see a previous attachment as more of a challenge than a barrier, mustn't he?"

Judith stood up, refusing to speak.

"Judith, I have offended you again," said Louisa-Margaretta, which was the closest she was likely to come to an apology. "But I am just trying to ensure that you do not repeat my mistake."

"Your mistake?" said Judith.

Louisa-Margaretta pointed at her stomach.

Judith gasped and fled the room.

Louisa-Margaretta gave a sigh, sitting down at her dressing table. Apparently, even the mention of her sin was enough to shock a rector's daughter! Not for the first time, she wished that Judith would show just a little bit more human weakness in her romantic attachments. Or perhaps she was beginning to favor Zharkov, and that was why she had run out. When it came to poor Cousin Morgan, Judith's spirit was certainly willing. If she could not live with a drawn-out engagement conducted across hundreds of miles, at least not when other eligible men were flinging themselves at her tired feet, well, she would not be the first to find herself giving in to temptation.

Louisa-Margaretta brought out her hand cream and began putting it on, ensuring that at least she would look well should they receive any other gentleman callers. Judith was so very maddening! She ought to have just married long before, then she would not have to think of such things. Judith would have to become a Quaker, of course, but Louisa-Margaretta had no doubt that the St Clairs would accept this change eventually. Judith had been engaged in secret, which was surprising but not terribly scandalous. And someday soon, Cousin Morgan would return from Vienna, then he and Judith would wed and spend their life in quiet contemplation and harsh moral judgement.

Louisa-Margaretta put down her hand cream and regarded her features critically. If she used just the barest bit of powder, so nobody could quite tell whether she had, that would be very becoming.

She might not have many friends in the cities, but if she could maintain the appearance of charming manners, she might yet find allies.

36

Louisa-Margaretta and Judith hardly exchanged a word at dinner, and even sharing the same room did not force them to speak. The next morning, Judith proposed a trip to visit Mr Solier with Mademoiselle Chatel and Madame Chatel. If Louisa-Margaretta was encouraging the attentions of that impoverished gentleman, it was high time they took advantage of it. Judith told the Cluetts that music was going to be a grand distraction. Mr Cluett, in particular, appeared not to believe her. But because they had a great deal of official business to take care of, they could not easily question her about it either.

They were forced to wait some time for Mademoiselle Marie, who had taken it into her head to attempt to look as pale and handsome as Louisa-Margaretta. This would never work, of course. The young lady, while healthy enough, did not have Miss Haddington's impressive features. But she would sit, fussing over her little curls and her dark hands, and try to look elegant.

When at last they were able to visit the young composer, he asked after the purpose of their call.

"Did you come just to listen to me play?" he said. "I must warn you, I am hard at work on another opera, and I cannot spare many moments away."

Judith could see Madame Chatel frowning with indignation. Unlike Mr Solier, she was very well established as an artist, and it was plain that she thought her minutes were even more valuable than his.

"No indeed," said Judith. "We do not require a great deal of time. We only have a little favor to ask."

He nodded, not at all curious. "I would like to have seen your friend, Miss Haddington. If it is not presumptuous to say so."

"Indeed not," said Judith while privately thinking that it was indeed very presumptuous. Then again, the gentleman in question was French, so she would endeavor to conform to his culture's curious behavior in this regard. "In fact, it was on behalf of my friend that I came today."

"Oh yes?" said the composer.

"I understand you are to give a concert in the palace," said Judith.

His face fell. "Yes, that is true. Just before the new year begins, there will be some entertainment."

"It is the talk of all Petersburg," said Mademoiselle Chatel, her eyes shining. "Oh, what a wonderful night it will be!"

Some coldness passed over the young man's face. "There are to be a great many composers. Why, I cannot think. I offered them three pieces of music commissioned specially for the occasion, yet they insist on snubbing me."

"You cannot worry yourself too greatly about their opinions," said Madame Chatel stoutly. "If you perform and your commissions are paid, best to get on with things."

The man sniffed. "I am not some tradesman, happy only

that his patrons have settled their account. If even the princes and princesses cannot appreciate true quality, I will have no choice but to leave Russia."

"That is better," said Mademoiselle Marie. "Goodness, how cold it is here, and how hopeless!"

"You have been before warm fires every day," snapped Madame Chatel. "Do not claim that I have neglected you."

Marie Chatel blinked. "I claimed nothing like that, *Mamon!*"

"Perhaps we could hear you play in the palace," said Judith hastily. "As you can see, the Russian winter has been rather trying for all of us. Do you think we might attend as your guests?"

The composer gave them a shrewd look. "Would Miss Haddington be in attendance?"

Judith smiled. Ever since Louisa-Margaretta had expressed alarm about her delicate condition by pointing at her own stomach, Judith had been determined to prove her worth as a matchmaker. Now, finally, she was beginning to succeed.

"She may come," said Judith. "In fact, I'm sure she can be relied upon if you need her to sing one of your beautiful arias."

37

Louisa-Margaretta frowned as she approached the home of some Russian nobleman whose name she couldn't remember, apparently a great friend of Monsieur Zharkov. She reflected that she herself ought to have been a Russian naval officer. Apparently, after the ice formed, they did almost nothing but go to balls and social events all winter. It was not easy to leave Petersburg in any sort of conveyance, so they were fortunate to be trapped in one of the most beautiful cities in the world.

For it *was* beautiful—Louisa-Margaretta now admitted as much. The snow was falling in the soft morning light, and soon, it would be dark again. The candlelight was festive, reminding Louisa-Margaretta of childhood Christmases with her brothers, when she had to worry about nothing more than which pony she would choose for her rides in the woods around their old home. Wycliff Castle, for all its rooms and rich furnishings, did not hold the same sort of memories. At least not for her. Though perhaps it would for her child, a thought that both amused and alarmed her.

Mr Cluett helped Louisa-Margaretta up the steps,

though she thought he seemed more likely to slip than she was. She always saw to it that her shoes were functional as well as stylish, though she wished she could be out riding instead of being forced to take carriages everywhere.

As luck would have it, Zharkov's host was just as dull as Mr Cluett, and he seemed content to pass the time speaking about Vienna. Louisa-Margaretta was rather impatient with all of those deliberations. If the diplomats could have done their job and carved up Europe more quickly, Cousin Morgan would have been able to leave. Perhaps then, Judith would be thinking more clearly, and Louisa-Margaretta wouldn't be forced to work out who was behind the attacks all on her own.

"Monsieur Zharkov, would you join me at the piano?" Louisa-Margaretta said, giving him a smile. Mr Cluett and the older man tactfully settled themselves into chairs nearer the fire, turning their backs on the young people. They had the wrong idea there, and Louisa-Margaretta found herself put out for a moment. If she had wished to marry a handsome bounder rather than a gentleman who combined good looks with good sense, she would have chosen someone like Zharkov many years before! But it suited her purposes not to be under terribly close observation. Let them think her a flirt.

"Would you like to hear me play, sir?" There was a sheet of music at the piano, and Louisa-Margaretta squinted at it. When she did begin to play it, she found that the melody was simple, but she still had trouble playing it at the required tempo. So she slowly plunked out the notes, her chords heavy and lolling, making just enough noise to cover up their conversation.

"I'm afraid Judith has spoiled me," said Louisa-

Margaretta, half to herself. "She is always playing, so I never do so anymore."

"Her playing is marvelous, indeed," said Monsieur Zharkov. "So methodical and yet so full of feeling."

Louisa-Margaretta glared at him. "Yes, well, it is high time you stopped listening to it."

Monsieur Zharkov only blinked at her. "Whatever do you mean?"

"Gossip is spreading about you and my friend Miss St Clair," she said haughtily. "It is high time you avoided her."

He frowned. "She has done nothing to expose herself to gossip."

"Except see rather too much of you," said Louisa-Margaretta. "A man who is known to be restless and far too interested in his military exploits to marry."

Monsieur Zharkov leaned closer. "If it were a question of marriage, I would resign my commission," he said with no hesitation in his voice. "For I have never met anyone like your friend Miss St Clair, and I am quite sure I never shall again."

Louisa-Margaretta gave a deep sigh. She recognised the irony of her position. How many times had she told her own mother that she would never find anyone like Isaac, and how true that had turned out to be! And yet here she sat, arguing the opposite to a heartsick young man.

"You could very well find someone else," she said, her fingers banging down on the keys. "Only you choose not to. What? Would you not be expected to marry well rather than choosing a penniless woman like Judith?"

"Miss St Clair's family is similar to mine. We spend time with the first families of Petersburg, but we are not *of* them, not quite. But while my family's pursuits have always included wealth, Miss St Clair seems quite untouched by such motives."

"Well," said Louisa-Margaretta, "*Miss* St Clair is soon to become *Mrs* Ramsbury, so however pure her heart, you ought not to be thinking such things, much less discussing them."

"Should she not be allowed to make her own decision?" Monsieur Zharkov said. "If she is, indeed, still certain of her fiancé, she can tell me herself. But if she wishes to marry elsewhere, I must tell her my feelings."

Louisa-Margaretta did not respond. If he was not in love with her friend, he was certainly an excellent actor. But she was not altogether sure that he had nothing to do with the attempts on the lives of the princes and princesses, for all that he had been sitting cozily with Judith during the first attack. Since all other approaches had failed, Louisa-Margaretta decided to be direct with the man.

"We have work to do here," she snapped. "And between us, Judith is meant to be the clever one. If she is thinking of nothing but chaperones and proposals of marriage, we shall never find this murderer."

"Murderer? I have not noticed a murder."

She was in no mood for his jests. "You know very well that one of the princes may have been killed. It was only luck that saved them both. I had the good luck not to die from that poison. But I would not expect that luck to hold."

He frowned. "Miss Haddington. I cannot imagine anyone trying to murder you. You do not even speak Russian. Nor do you have any great knowledge about our royal family."

"Well then," she said, laboring over the next passage. If only Judith were here to play! But she could not stop, otherwise the gentlemen across the room might hear.

"Do enlighten me, Monsieur Zharkov. What is it about the royal family that would lead someone to try and murder them, one by one? What have you not been telling me?"

He looked as if he would consider it for a moment, and he paused before speaking again. "I would advise you to avoid the palace as well as any contact with the family. If you are correct about this murderer, it must be nearly certain that the next attack will take place there."

"Avoid the palace," murmured Louisa-Margaretta. "What an interesting idea."

She smiled up at him, aware that she was missing half the notes, then set the composition aside. "Thank you for telling me more about your charming city," she said loudly, grinning more widely this time. "You are a wonderful host, but you must be eager to resume your travels."

Monsieur Zharkov, poor fool, was plainly the sort of man who could not do without traveling. He went on a great deal about his plans for the following summer, and Louisa-Margaretta smiled to herself. He must really have believed her vague assurances. He hadn't noticed that she had made no promises.

For she was not going to avoid the palace.

She was going to storm it.

38

Catherine Pavlovna had no smile on her face as she listened to the first of Mr Solier's compositions, a strange musical number that seemed to combine a solemn Russian folk tune with a great many French flourishes.

Princess Catherine, of course, was sitting in the front. Judith, near the very back of the crowd, shifted so that she could keep the princess in her view. She would never grow used to the grandeur of the palace, the many ornaments and decorations that gave its ballrooms an almost terrifying opulence.

The murderer had tried to harm the two youngest princes, then they had gone for Anna Pavlovna. Catherine, as the next eldest, was at the greatest risk. After that, the individual might very well attack Konstantin Pavlovich, and after that, perhaps even Emperor Alexander. He was, presumably, safe in Vienna at this moment, but the attacker might well seek him out.

Judith's fingers, stiff in her best gloves, made her uncomfortable as she watched the crowd. Someone among them must wish very great harm on the royal family, but she was still not able to figure out who it was.

And she knew very well that she was running out of time.

Monsieur Solier had needed no persuasion to have Louisa-Margaretta sing one of his arias. There were Russian singers who were more highly skilled, but few could match Louisa-Margaretta's command of the fiery libretto. As it turned out, Mr Solier had one number that featured a lady nearly as furious as Medea. The general message of the words was that the man who had wronged her would be made to pay a great price.

It was, Judith thought sadly, a message that Louisa-Margaretta must have longed to deliver to the man who was the natural father of her child. But Judith herself knew all of the complications of that situation, and she could not greatly fault either her friend or the gentleman. They had sinned, to be sure, but no more than many, and the price that Louisa-Margaretta had already paid was exceptionally high. If she continued courting Monsieur Solier, who made no secret of preferring his own melodies to any woman or man he had ever met, that price would be higher still.

Most of the crowd appeared very interested, but there were a few who would go about gossiping like peasants at an opera. Judith was surprised to find that one of them was the youngest princess.

"I'm glad to find you here, Miss St Clair," said Anna Pavlovna. "My sister is terrible company."

Judith cleared her throat. She could not very well insult a princess like Catherine Pavlovna, but if she did not say anything at all, the other princess would be offended.

"Having a sister can be trying at times," she said delicately. "I am not always the best of friends with my own sister, though I miss her now. With more distant relations, such as cousins, I've found things rather easier. But then, one does not have quite the same friendship there either."

Anna Pavlovna glared up at the stage. "Miss Haddington is enjoying herself," she said bitterly.

Judith, who could not follow the princess's train of thought at all, was surprised. "Oh, I am sure she is just honored to be able to contribute to the evening."

It was as if she had not spoken. "Catherine did not like my gown," said Anna Pavlovna. "But my brothers thought it very becoming!"

"And so it is," said Judith immediately. But their conversation was interrupted by the end of the aria.

The audience applauded, not only with politeness but with true enthusiasm. Judith could see that Louisa-Margaretta's face was glowing, suffused with triumph. She wondered about all of the tales she always heard. A woman who expected joy in some future month was sometimes said to be ugly and other times to have a beauty that was transcendent. In Louisa-Margaretta's case, beauty had clearly won out. Mr Solier kept smiling at her.

Perhaps it was not all to do with money, then. Perhaps there might be the beginnings of love. Judith smiled to herself, thinking that she had helped bring about this happy occasion.

But when she looked again, Anna Pavlovna had left. And Catherine Pavlovna was in danger of being swallowed by the elegantly dressed crowd.

Judith looked over at the Chatel pair. Both mother and daughter appeared distressed. They had been at odds more than ever lately, and Judith wondered whether they would go to England together or if Marie would wish to live with a different family.

Something in the conversation with Anna Pavlovna was staying in Judith's mind. The princess, without meaning to, had helped Judith work out the identity of the killer.

And, after looking about the crowded ballroom, she saw the person leaving. Judith took one last look around her, but there was nobody who could help. Louisa-Margaretta had disappeared.

She would have to go alone.

39

Mr Solier kept receiving congratulations from all quarters, and Louisa-Margaretta's conversation was hardly less celebrated. She finally hissed for him to come over to the edge of the little ensemble of musicians. They were between numbers now in the performance, but they were still playing as servants rushed about, preparing the grand space for dancing.

"Go on, then," he said. "What did you wish to say to me, Miss Haddington?"

It was not clear whether he was ignorant or simply acting modest. Louisa-Margaretta knew that she should not have such a sensitive conversation in a palace. But she was still within view of a great deal of people, so there should be no scandal about it.

"I must marry soon," she said. "My parents cannot give their blessing, so I must hope that the Cluetts' blessing will serve."

"And if it does not?" said the gentleman.

He did not have to ask whether Louisa-Margaretta

would receive her fortune if her parents did not agree to the match.

"It will," she said, with more conviction than she felt. "My parents dote on their grandchildren, and they will wish to provide for my child."

He looked about them. "We must have a house in London, then. To own the truth, England has never been my favorite country. But how I could write, if only I did not have to think about scraping for every kopeck!"

Louisa-Margaretta tried not to let tears come to her eyes. While she knew that all marriages had some consideration for the precise sum each party might contribute, she had always thought that entering into an engagement would be at least pleasant. But she felt like a kitchen maid at a market, trying to buy carrots with ready money.

"You do not look happy, Miss Haddington," he said. "But it is for the best. I am not such a terrible choice, surely! Not many young ladies are able to say that they have married one of the greatest geniuses of a generation."

He was quite sincere, and Louisa-Margaretta almost laughed, though her throat still felt heavy. She saw the Chatels quarreling and noticed that Vladilena Maximovna was approaching one of the princesses. Mr Kuzmin was laughing at something the Dutch ambassador had said, though his expression was unsettled.

Louisa-Margaretta took a deep breath. She had come to St Petersburg to find a husband, and now, she had succeeded. Though her entire body felt tired and empty, she mustn't think of that now, not when so many lives were at risk.

"So, it is settled, then?" said Mr Solier. "Only I am afraid half the city seems to think that matchmaking is wise, and I spent a great deal of time talking to Russian young ladies whose mamas have some interest in music. Were an engagement to become generally known, I would have more time to myself. And I was thinking my next opera ought to be set in Paris—"

"Did you have a question for me, then?" asked Louisa-Margaretta sharply.

It was then that she saw Judith leaving.

"I am sorry," she said. "I must run after my friend!"

And she went, not very elegantly, without another second to think about her plans.

40

The figure was walking quickly to the cathedral, Judith realised. It was a beautiful space within the palace, more ornate than anything Judith had ever seen outside it. For a moment, she wished she could be within it and simply appreciate the majesty. Although philosophically, she agreed with plain Quaker meeting houses and the drafty stone churches of her childhood, this space was beautiful.

But she had to speak with the figure in front of her. "Do not harm Catherine," she said. She had spoken, without thinking, in English. She tried to change to Russian.

The woman turned. "Whyever would I harm her?" she said. "It is Konstantin I mean to kill."

Louisa-Margaretta arrived. "You have been killing all the princes," she said, breathing hard from running but with more spirit than Judith had seen in months.

Mary Josefa's scowl was unlike any expression Judith had ever seen on her features.

"I did not have any luck with those two," she said. "But they were humiliated, and that was good enough. I was waiting for my target, and if some fools thought I was trying to assassinate the whole family, that was perfectly fine."

Louisa-Margaretta was shaking her head, but Judith's memories had become clear.

"Miss Claudio, your cousin," she said. "She was in the front room with me during the first attack. I suppose she sent you some kind of signal. If she is really your cousin, that is."

"She is my sister," said Mary Josefa. "And her real name, of course, is not Miss Claudio. Neither is mine. I took that from Shakespeare."

"What?" said Louisa-Margaretta, as Judith said, quoting the line, "'Kill Claudio?'"

"Yes," said Mary Josefa. "But this is no silly comedy, of course. Revenge is rather serious."

"Revenge for what?" said Louisa-Margaretta.

Mary Josefa pulled a knife from her cloak, and Judith stumbled backwards.

"Listen," said Mary Josefa. "I do not wish to harm either of you two ladies. But when you hear what Konstantin Pavlovich did, you will stop trying to stand in the way of my plans."

Judith looked at Louisa-Margaretta. "Very well," she said quietly.

Mary Josefa gave a dark smile. "My sister was a beautiful woman. Unfortunately, Konstantin Pavlovich also thought so. And in refusing him, she brought about her own death."

Judith, in spite of Louisa-Margaretta's hand on her arm, moved towards the cloaked figure. "I am very sorry for your loss," she said solemnly.

"As am I," said Louisa-Margaretta, "but upon my soul, that is no reason to kill his whole family!"

"Nobody has been killed," said Mary Josefa primly. "And nobody will die, apart from Konstantin Pavlovich."

"Please," said Judith. "Mary Josefa, you of all people must understand! You must think of your own soul."

"Why did you try to poison the princess, then?" said Louisa-Margaretta.

Mary Josefa laughed. "I am not a fool. I knew that nobody would die. But I did hope the two of you might stop trying to ruin my plans before the main event."

Louisa-Margaretta stared at her. "You might have poisoned any of the Kutuzova girls!"

"And why should I not?" hissed Mary Josefa. "Their father investigated what happened to my sister. Some investigation! Konstantin Pavlovich should have been executed for what he did to her, and yet he was let off with nothing."

There were footsteps, and Mary Josefa looked about her.

"If you give me the knife," said Judith, "we can walk out peacefully. We shall pretend that we were lost."

When Mary Josefa handed it to her, Judith felt terrified to be holding the dagger, and she had no place to hide it as Mary Josefa had. She looked about for some sort of disguise, finally settling on one of the handkerchiefs she kept with her.

"Give it to me," snapped Louisa-Margaretta, who was holding a small bag. Judith knew her friend had brought pieces of paper with the words she was to sing scrawled on them, though she had not ended up needing those. Louisa-Margaretta had an excellent memory for libretti.

"Ladies!" said Mr Solier. "I hope you are done with your prayers. Otherwise, you will miss all the dancing."

"Most of our prayers have been answered," said Mary Josefa, though Judith saw a tear twinkling in her eye. "God is very good to us."

They walked out in a strange procession. Mr Solier accompanied them, but because Mr Cluett was with them the whole time, their conversation was of no substance. When they reached the ballroom, Judith was relieved that Louisa-Margaretta asked to go home. Mary Josefa, whom Judith could not look at, also melted away.

It was not until they made their way upstairs at the Cluetts', prepared to sleep, and let the tired maids put away their best gowns, that Louisa-Margaretta realised the knife was no longer in her cloak.

And by then, it was too late.

41

Louisa-Margaretta did not much like the surname of Solier. She did not like thinking of herself as a Solier.

However, some part of her could imagine her child as a little Solier, and without thinking, her hands flew to her stomach. She would need to choose a name before spring. And no matter how difficult the marriage might be, the confinement would draw near regardless of the family circumstances. She took some comfort in that.

With some unease, she settled herself on the bed. The doctor was coming to examine her, at Judith's insistence. They had told the Cluetts it was to be sure there were no lingering effects from her earlier illness, but Louisa-Margaretta imagined their hosts must have guessed the truth. Whatever they knew, though, they did not say directly. They were good diplomats.

Vladilena Maximovna spoke to Louisa-Margaretta briskly throughout the examination, but there was kindness in her face. "I won't hurt you," she said, and she described exactly what she wished to do before she did it. Louisa-Margaretta, in spite of herself, began to feel a little bit better. If anything were amiss, the doctor would be able to tell her.

But the question she heard was not what she expected.

"Now," said the doctor, sitting at the end of the bed. "Please tell me what it was that convinced you to plan for a child's birth at the end of spring, Miss Haddington."

Louisa-Margaretta could hardly speak. "What do you want to know, then? Surely you cannot expect me to give you details?"

The doctor shook her head once. "No. No details, please. I do not need to know anything about what scared you into thinking you *might* have a child. I know that well enough. What convinced you that you *would* have a child?"

Louisa-Margaretta shifted. "Each month, there is nothing," she said crisply. "I am not so naive as to mistake the meaning of that."

"Not naive, but mistaken," said the doctor gently. "There will be no confinement. You are not with child."

This was evidently not the first time she had delivered this piece of news, for she moved closer and made as if to catch Louisa-Margaretta. Instead of fainting, the younger woman got up from the bed and stood glaring down at the doctor.

"That is not possible," she said, insistent. "It is not just the absence of—of blood! I have been exhausted, and yet I sleep poorly. My whole body feels ill, and I was always healthy. I have sick headaches, and I never had them before, not once in my life."

When Vladilena Maximovna did not respond right away, a frisson of fear ran through Louisa-Margaretta. "I am ill," she said. "That is it, isn't it? Tell me whether I am to die."

The doctor went over to Louisa-Margaretta's dressing table. She rummaged through its contents, much more carelessly than any maid would have, and took out the cream that Louisa-Margaretta had been using. The vinegary concoction stank when she opened the jar.

"You have been using this?" said the doctor, striding over to Louisa-Margaretta, who had seated herself on the bed.

Louisa-Margaretta nodded primly. "I was always outdoors when we lived in Derbyshire," she said. "My hands got terribly brown whenever I forgot my gloves."

The doctor's eyes narrowed, and she dropped the cream in the large bag she had brought with her. "Well, you shall have to let them stay brown. There is far too much lead in this cream. Avoid it, and you may expect a full recovery."

Louisa-Margaretta shook her head. "Many English ladies use lead in different forms. It has a lovely effect on the skin."

"And it has been recognised, for millennia, as a poison," snapped the doctor. "Truly, Miss Haddington, you must allow that I have experience and knowledge well beyond yours. Leave off the cream and any powders, and you will never make this mistake again. You seem well enough, so without the poison, it should not be long until you make a complete recovery."

A knock came at the door as Louisa-Margaretta was turning this explanation over in her mind, wondering whether it could be true. She did not doubt that she was not carrying a child, though she was surprised by the weight of the disappointment. But a cream, and one used by a great deal of ladies? It seemed fantastical that it could have given her such trouble.

"Come in," she said rather absently, and Judith entered.

She was too wise to ask directly, but Louisa-Margaretta pointed to herself.

"It was nothing," she said. "There is no baby. There never was."

She was surprised by what a struggle it was to say the words. Louisa-Margaretta had always supposed herself unaffected by the infant she had been forced to carry, but at some point, her resignation about her own condition had carried a hint of joy. Now, it was all to be forgotten.

"I am very sorry," said Judith, going to sit by her friend.

Vladilena Maximovna closed her bag and moved towards the door. "I am sure we will meet again soon," she said.

Louisa-Margaretta smiled faintly. "Are you? I am not." Remembering Judith's description of the shadowy gathering of women, she wondered whether the doctor would have anything to do with two English women who refused to help promote any radical changes to the Russian government. She felt slightly ashamed of having spent nearly every waking hour preparing for a birth that would not come to pass.

"I believe I heard something about what passed at the palace after we left," said Judith carefully. "Could you enlighten us?"

The other woman came to sit on the bed again, and she lowered her voice. "There was a story," the doctor said. "Konstantin Pavlovich was nearly mad with fear. He ran all about the palace, saying that some woman had cut off his finger and threatened to kill him. Because I was in attendance at the ball, but no other doctor was nearby, they sent for me to stop the bleeding."

Louisa-Margaretta was silent, but Judith spoke.

"Why did this person not kill him?" Judith said. She paused a moment. "If, of course, one can believe his story."

"Well," said the doctor. "Only an hour later, Prince Konstantin changed his story and claimed that he had no idea why anyone would wish to harm him. But what he said as I was dressing the wound was that he wished to become a monk. 'If this spectre of death will only leave me, I shall become a monk,' he kept repeating."

"Do you think he will?" said Louisa-Margaretta boldly. "Become a monk, I mean?"

The doctor paused then said, "Perhaps not precisely. But he seemed well aware of the dangers of his present course and terrified for his life. And he has not been at all well since then, though I am no longer concerned about the wound."

Louisa-Margaretta did not say anything else. Men like the prince were too often left to do whatever they wished in the world, without regard for others, so she felt it would be far too optimistic to hope for another ending. And yet perhaps she would be proved wrong, especially if Konstantin's military judgement continued to be unreliable.

They were interrupted by another knock. The doctor cleared her throat and called the visitors in.

It turned out to be not only both Madame and Mademoiselle Chatel but also Mrs Cluett. Their faces were most grave.

"Miss St Clair," said Mrs Cluett. "We have just had a letter."

Louisa-Margaretta looked at Judith, who had risen to her feet. She must have caught something in the tone or in the fact that all the ladies were descending on her together.

"It is bad news," said Judith, standing perfectly still.

"Yes," said Mrs Cluett, but she seemed unable to go on.

Mademoiselle Chatel flew over to the bed and took Judith's hand, drawing her down until she was seated. "Dear Judith," she said. "Your Mr Ramsbury was escorting another diplomat back to England." She paused.

Louisa-Margaretta glared at her. "Out with it, then!"

"He is killed?" said Judith.

"No," said Madame Chatel. "No, dear child. But he is missing."

AFTERWORD

My deepest apologies to all of the historical figures who have been placed in this book. It should not be taken as a faithful representation of history, though the names and ages of the royal family members are accurate.

Konstantin Pavlovich did, indeed, murder a woman called Madame Araujo. As far as I could learn, he never faced any consequences for these actions, though Kutuzov did make an attempt to investigate. He died years later of cholera.

My deepest thanks to all of the many friends, family members, and complete strangers who helped with the historical research for this book. I can't thank you enough!

Note: For a free prequel novella and access to our newsletter, please visit www.tenaciousteacuppress.com/eveTnews.

TWO LADIES AND A MANHUNT

1

Note: For a free and complete copy of this prequel novella, join our newsletter here.

Louisa-Margaretta Haddington stood perfectly still, listening to a torrent of endearments and praise.

"Your beauty, Miss Haddington, can be compared only to the absolute perfection of your mind. You are the epitome of culture and grace, and I should not consider myself the least bit worthy of asking for your hand in marriage, were it not for one thing."

She could hear no more. "Really, I hardly think—"

"Hear me out. No man on earth could possibly be worthy of you, and since you must marry, I may as well ask. Why not choose me? For I certainly have several things to recommend me, though I would not propose to think myself your equal. For you are ever so divine—"

"Stop." Though she tried to look cross, she could not keep herself from laughing. "I am sure you are very wrong."

Louisa-Margaretta was tall, and though the praise for her beauty may have been exaggerated, it was still not far from the truth. Her tresses were reddish gold, her complexion radiant, her eyes lively. Her figure spoke to both perfect health and regular exercise, and all that was helped along by a surfeit of confidence. If Louisa-Margaretta had doubts, they were never about her own worth but only that of others.

Her friend Miss Lavinia Finch had been lying on the sofa, but she sat up and took a sip of tea. Though she had also been laughing as she professed her undying love for Louisa-Margaretta, she began to frown. After taking another lump of sugar, she stirred it into her tea. "Mr Fudge is far from stupid, in spite of his unfortunate name," she said. "You would be a fool not to consider his proposal."

Abandoning her tea, Louisa-Margaretta walked over to the pianoforte and began to play an etude. Though her technique was imperfect, she made up for it in the vivacity of her performance. "There has been no proposal," she said. "It would be improper before I am out."

Lavinia raised her eyebrows at her friend. "After tomorrow, you *will* be out."

Louisa-Margaretta sighed. "Yes, we shall both be out, I suppose. And I would rather die than be the next Mrs Fudge."

Glaring, Lavinia replied, "I am sure you would not wish to die, Louisa-Margaretta. There are many worse things than marrying an honourable man such as Mr Fudge."

Louisa-Margaretta switched to an aria, though she did not sing it. In truth, it was hard for her to imagine something worse than marrying Mr Christmas Fudge. He was twenty years older than her, not at all handsome, and a dear friend of both her parents. *At eighteen, am I to be a stepmother to his three children?* She could not bear even entertaining such an idea.

"You marry him, then," she said. "If you are willing to be Mrs Fudge, I shall wish you joy."

Lavinia was still glaring. "He has not offered any attentions to me, nor is he like to." And with that, she walked out of the room without a single word of goodbye.

"Did Lavinia leave so soon?" Louisa-Margaretta's mother asked, walking in and frowning at the tea things. "I wished to speak with her about tomorrow."

"Yes." Louisa-Margaretta had been answering Mama with only one word for days, and she was not going to give her any more information.

"Louisa-Margaretta." Mrs Haddington sat down next to her daughter. "I am sure that you may feel rather vexed, but ruining the reputation of our family is not the balm you are seeking. You must be polite to our callers, and tomorrow, you must put on your best smile at court. One does not snub the queen."

"Yes," said Louisa-Margaretta again. In truth, she had no quarrel with the queen, and she would not have any trouble with Mr Fudge if he did not insist on admiring her.

"Darling, if you will not listen to me, look to God for guidance."

"Yes," said Louisa-Margaretta again before escaping.

2

———————

"These things are sent to try us," murmured Judith St Clair to her cousin Dorothy St Clair.

"It is not trying," said Dorothy. "Never, because I am not going to be defeated! I shall not accept it, Judith."

Tears of anger were streaking down her face. Judith, who was used to comforting people who grieved, found herself perplexed.

Of course, Judith's younger sister, Miriam, often cried over life's smaller trials. But ever since they had arrived in London for a visit, little Miriam had spent much of her time with their young cousin Rollo. At eleven, Miriam liked ribbons, but she was not interested in the talk of balls and coming out. She would rather run about with Dorothy's youngest brother, enjoying the sights of the city street from the window and getting paint on her best frock during their artistic endeavours.

"I am sure there are partners aplenty to be found outside of Almack's." Judith hated dancing and felt relieved that the most prestigious location in London was very far out of her reach.

"Not the sort of partner I would wish to marry," said Dorothy, sobbing again.

Judith tried a little pat on the shoulder then murmured some words of comfort before abandoning her cousin. If she kept trying to soothe her companion, she would likely say something that revealed her complete indifference.

When Judith sought solitude in her parents' room, her mother tried to rise from the bed. "I am sorry, dear," she said. "I should have been the one to comfort Dorothy."

"Her mother should do it." Judith knew she should not grumble, but as she took her mother's hand, she felt both more petulant and more comfortable.

"One of us should," said Mrs St Clair. "But as none of us had any expectations from Almack's, it is hard to know exactly what to tell her."

Judith's mother had carried at least three children since Miriam's birth but given birth to none. She had passed the time when things seemed to go wrong. Still, Judith was anxious and chastised herself for upsetting her mother.

"What is it, dear?" asked her mama gently. "You can tell me, you know. You and your father have been tiptoeing about for months. Only Miriam tells me things now."

Judith swallowed. She wished she could have told her father, but even with his gentle nature, she was quite sure he would not understand.

"I don't wish to be out," she said. "Oh, Mama, I feel the same as I did last year. Must I accompany Dorothy to balls?"

Mama sighed. "Yes. You are nineteen now, Judith. And your cousin is depending on you."

Judith turned away. She refused to argue more, but she

could not imagine throwing herself into the world that Dorothy seemed to take for granted. The harsh conversations about wealth, birth, and childbearing prospects that she had heard her whole life seemed entirely apart from what she wished. It all seemed so very unholy. *How can my parents, who raised me to love and respect God and my fellow man, go in for such a thing?*

"Mama," she said.

But her mother shook her head. "You must be kind to Dorothy. She's had a very trying year, watching all her brothers and sisters leave."

Judith left the room. Of course Dorothy had been going through a trying time, but it didn't follow that Judith must be thrown into a marriage market so merciless that it was sure to make her own year equally trying. At least, she hoped not.

3

───────

"Lou, you must be kind to Christmas, now," said her father. "He's had a trying year."

The Haddingtons were all gathered in their sitting room, as they had gotten word that Mr Fudge was going to call. Mr and Mrs Haddington as well as their son Sherborne were happily anticipating the visit.

"I have had a trying year myself," said Louisa-Margaretta. Perhaps it was not fair, but she found herself being gentle with her father, though he had the same annoying demands as Mama. "Why is there no sympathy for the sort of year I have had? Dragged to London for the season, deprived of my horses, forced to parade about in all sorts of silly clothing."

Papa only laughed. "Very silly," he agreed, chortling. "The hoops!"

Louisa-Margaretta saw her opening. Her father agreed that the ceremony of being presented at court was ridiculous. Perhaps she could enlist him, and they could talk Mama out of that particular requirement.

Mr Fudge's voice put the idea out of her mind. He had

entered the room and was greeting everyone warmly. She had to stop herself from sticking her tongue out at him. For years, they had gotten on well, as her fondness for the hunt and for her brother's constant games of cricket had amused him. Now she could hardly bring herself to look at him.

"It is wonderful to see you, Christmas," said Mama. "I trust we may see a great deal of each other now that we are back in London." Their country house was not twenty miles outside the city, but Mama always talked about it as if it were worlds away.

"I very much hope so," he said. His voice was low and gentle. Mr Fudge was one of the few people whose manners never seemed to change or slip. He was always polite, never condescending.

"I was hoping to see you all at Almack's... perhaps the day after tomorrow?" Though he addressed the group, it was plain that Lousia-Margaretta's company was his greatest interest.

Louisa-Margaretta's father grinned. "No. I'm afraid not."

Mr Fudge drew in a breath, and for a moment, the attention was away from Louisa-Margaretta.

"Not again," said Mr Fudge mildly.

"Yes!" answered Papa, sounding delighted. "Every year, in fact."

Sherbourne, who hated dancing and avoided Almack's as a rule, looked extremely confused. "What is every year?"

"They don't let Papa go," said Louisa-Margaretta. "It's a way of punishing Mama for not marrying where those harpies thought she should."

"Louisa-Margaretta. Honestly, you know your father would rather not attend. And I, myself, would prefer to be in church. But because it is your season—"

"Keep Papa out?" asked Sherborne. Of all the

Haddington children, he looked most like his father. But his brown hair was thicker, his dark eyes more arrogant. He had always wanted to be his father's partner in business but much preferred London to Manchester. Though he liked to think he was just as practical as his father, who had grown up poor, he was a product of his comfortable upbringing.

Mr Fudge shook his head. "It really is unconscionable, the way they split up families. If you would like me to have a word?"

"They wouldn't listen to even a magistrate, my dear," said Mama. "And truly, we need to stay in favour for our Louisa-Margaretta's sake. Otherwise, I would consider having a word myself."

"Harpies," said Sherbourne, which earned him a hard look from both his parents. "What? I'm sure they don't even know everyone by sight. If I were to go with one of my poorest friends from Oxford but dress him up in expensive clothing and claim he was a cousin, I am quite sure they would admit us."

"The day after tomorrow sounds delightful," said Mama pointedly. "Sherbourne, I am sure you will join us in your father's place. As I mentioned, it is important for your sister."

Sherbourne looked mutinous, and Louisa-Margaretta was secretly delighted that two of her parents' children were cross with them at once. Augustus was the only other Haddington staying at the London home, but he was to be married in two weeks and spent many hours with his bride.

"I can't think of a worse place in London," he said. "Nothing good to eat or drink and the worst possible company." After a pause, he added, "Meaning no offence, I'm sure, Mr Fudge."

"None taken," said their visitor, sitting and smiling at them all.

Louisa-Margaretta tried to keep herself from groaning. She could hardly tell which thing she dreaded more, being presented at court or being forced into an evening of dancing with Mr Fudge.

4

———

Louisa-Margaretta and Lavinia shared a carriage. It had been arranged beforehand that their mothers would arrive separately, as the costumes the girls were wearing were so large as to make sharing the confined space impossible for more than two young ladies. And though Louisa-Margaretta had better friends, she had always gotten on well with Lavinia until the day before.

She was not one to apologise, but Lavinia did not share that characteristic.

"Louisa-Margaretta," she said, "I'm sorry I was cross with you yesterday."

Their carriage was admitted to the grounds of the palace, perhaps at the very moment when even the most confident young lady might start to feel some nerves at the idea of being in Queen Charlotte's presence.

"You still seem rather cross," said Louisa-Margaretta, not looking at her friend.

"Yes, well, these circumstances would be trying for a better woman," said Lavinia, a pained look on her face.

Louisa-Margaretta examined her own costume and sighed. The hoops were large, the fabric distinctly uncomfortable. White crepe with a good deal of lace and ornamentation, it was the sort of garment that begged for a stain. She wondered when she was going to be able to eat another meal.

"These hoops shouldn't be so large," she murmured, trying to push hers into a better shape. "I feel ridiculous."

"We're fortunate they are," said Lavinia darkly. "We can all look equally ridiculous. Lord, what a silly show."

"Are you not happy to be seeing Queen Charlotte?" asked Louisa-Margaretta. Though she was dreading the spectacle, she would have thought her old friend might enjoy such a thing. Lavinia had always spoken of any brushes with royalty with great reverence.

"Perhaps I would be," she said tonelessly. "Tell me... What would you think if you knew this were the last time you would ever see this palace?"

Louisa-Margaretta had been distracted, thinking of how much time she would have to spend in the dull charade before she could beg her mother to leave, and the question sounded odd to her. "Lavinia, what do you mean?"

But the moment had passed. Lavinia was gazing out at the palace walls, waiting for the carriage to stop so she could step out. "Forget what I said. It is of no consequence."

Louisa-Margaretta frowned. "I wish you would tell me."

She would forget that conversation after, in the bustle of the presentation and her curiosity about the other men and women who were presented to Queen Charlotte. She had heard a rumour that the king was unwell, but they all had a chance to see him. And he did not look terribly indisposed as he cut a cake that was fully six feet tall, to the gasped admiration of the crowd.

She ought to have asked Lavinia what she meant. Later, she would have great cause to regret not doing so.

5

____

Louisa-Margaretta had begged her mother to take her shopping. If she were to go dancing, at least she could wear the worst dress she could possibly find —something that would send a message to a suitor like Mr Fudge and would put him off her forever. At Queen Charlotte's ball the day before, he had hoped to dance with her, but she had retreated to a different room with what she claimed were nerves. Her mother had not been fooled, but unwilling to make a scene, Mrs Haddington had accepted the excuse. In the morning, she chastised her daughter, letting her know plainly that they would never go back to the country unless Louisa-Margaretta made an effort in London.

She could not have thought of any argument better suited to forcing her only daughter into compliance. Louisa-Margaretta, determined to dance, joined her mother in a dressmaker's shop while her father and brother went to call on an acquaintance.

"I think that black would suit me," Louisa-Margaretta said. "Something like this."

The garment she had found was a worsted day dress made in a very deep grey. It might have done well for a widow, but she would be laughed out of a ballroom.

Mama was not fooled for an instant. "You are not wearing such a thing to Almack's. I don't know why we came. Look, there are Papa and Sherbourne waiting in the carriage. If this is what you had in mind for a purchase, we may as well go join them."

They left the shop empty-handed. Papa stepped out of the carriage and handed up his wife then followed Louisa-Margaretta back in after helping her up.

"I'm not sure why I must be forced to wear something in a gay colour," said Louisa-Margaretta as her mother began murmuring something to Papa about the horrid ball they were supposed to hold in her honour.

"White is a symbol of death in many countries," said Sherborne. "You could go in white muslin in a funereal sense."

Louisa-Margaretta pouted. "I shall be forced to go in white muslin," she said. "But I won't do any dancing."

A family passed their carriage. It consisted of a handsome woman, the roundness of her belly not quite perfectly concealed under a light gown and a coat, a pretty young daughter, and a plainer, dark-haired daughter about Louisa-Margaretta's age. Louisa-Margaretta smiled. So sour did the older daughter look as she was steered into the shop by her mother. They looked too poor to have to worry about Almack's, but the pressure for a good marriage was nearly universal for young women. As was the resistance to it, apparently.

Louisa-Margaretta looked over to see her father holding his head in his hands, her mother looking grim.

"Papa!" she said, shocked. Her father, as a rule, did not believe in illness.

"It's nothing," he managed, looking at her. "A headache."

"Anyone could get a headache from waiting in front of shops all day," said Sherborne. "Let's go home. We must all be fresh for the evening."

Though he had meant to tell a joke, Louisa-Margaretta could not help but agree.

6

Judith entered the shop with Miriam and her mother, as Dorothy had practically run ahead of them. Judith looked more closely at a dark-grey worsted, but Dorothy dragged her away.

"Don't be dull," she said. "That would never do for the season!"

"It would make a very good day dress," said Judith.

"Of course not. Oh, Judith! You would look ever so plain."

Judith looked to her mother for support, but Mrs St Clair looked very pale. She was touching the wall as if she would faint.

The dressmaker, likely taking note of her condition, found her a chair. "There you are, dearie. Don't try to get up too soon. Sarah!" she said, raising her voice without shouting. "Smelling salts for the lady!"

Mrs St Clair blinked. She usually hated when people fussed over her, even though the talk of her confinement made it more likely. But she settled into the chair and even sniffed the smelling salts twice. "Yes, thank you."

Dorothy, not at all concerned for her aunt, had found a beautiful dress in yellow silk. It would have looked terrible with Judith's thin dark hair but would probably flatter Dorothy.

"This one is lovely," she said, trying to pull Judith over.

"Dorothy," snapped Judith. "I must see to Mama."

"Judith." Her mother took her hand. "You are the most precious gift in the world to me and to Papa. Did you know that? You and Miriam."

It was a sentiment that Judith often heard from her mother, but rarely did a dressmaker's shop inspire such reflections. She frowned, wondering if Mama was feeling well and whether they ought to all leave at that instant to return home.

"Shall we go, Mama?" she asked.

"No, dear. Dorothy wanted to see the dresses. When she is content to leave, we must all walk back together."

Judith sighed. She was glad to hear her mother's voice returning to its usual vivacious pitch but felt that if she saw another series of lacy gowns, she would fall asleep from the tedium of boring luxuries that her family could not possibly afford.

7

"I shall never again wear lace," said Louisa-Margaretta. Her favourite fan had caught on her gown again, and as she tried to yank it free, she tore some of the lace.

Mama peered at it. "You will have to mend it yourself," she said, shaking her head. "If we were to return home now, we would miss half the dancing."

"I can't mend it. You know my skills with a needle go no further than holding it in my hand as I make conversation."

Mama sighed. "Your last two governesses were supposed to teach you, darling. For just such an occasion."

"Yes, well, they both failed to do so."

"Undoubtedly because their pupil was particularly unwilling to learn."

"Undoubtedly."

She gazed miserably over at Sherborne, who had been uncharacteristically gay the whole evening. It might have had something to do with the very well-dressed friend who had accompanied him. Louisa-Margaretta noted with a pang that her brother's friend was exceedingly handsome and wondered why they had not been introduced. Indeed, now that she had been presented at court, it would be proper for her to dance with such a young man, and she was surprised to find herself thrilled by the thought. For not only was he handsome, but he had something about him which drew and held her attention. It was the same, she realised, as happened at the theatre. Those who were most captivating on the stage did not always have the greatest beauty. But that young man, it appeared, had been gifted with both.

Without being told, Louisa-Margaretta covered the tear in the lace with her elbow. It might look frayed, but it was not large enough to attract undue attention in the crowded assembly room at Almack's. Besides, she knew that she had beauty enough that such a thing ought not to detract from it.

"Miss Haddington" came a voice before them, and she did not even think of suppressing a sigh as she turned.

"Christmas," her mother said, even more than her usual warmth flowing into her greeting.

"Mr Fudge." Louisa-Margaretta would not lie to him and say that she was pleased to see him.

"Miss Haddington. I trust you enjoyed yourself at court. Might I ask for the next two dances, if you are not otherwise engaged?"

"Yes," said Mama. "We have only just arrived. And I shall be delighted to see your very superior dancing."

"You are too kind. I know you would rather be else-where, but I am glad that you are playing chaperone to our dear Miss Haddington."

Mama's eyes sparkled. "How well you know me! Yes, my religious work is important to me, but so, too, are my dear children."

Louisa-Margaretta longed for a retort, but the music finished, and she was forced to take her place with Mr Fudge.

At least he was a precise dancer and a silent one. Though he was not often in gay company, she noticed that he remembered all the steps and executed them well. Indeed, he had an excellent memory, something that she had often remarked upon when he was simply a friend of her parents who liked to visit their household. But ever since he had begun making sheep's eyes at her, conversation had been out of the question.

"How are you enjoying your season in London, Miss Haddington?" he asked eventually. "I hope you have been comfortable here."

"In the city?" she asked. "Never. I suppose the theatre is not the worst amusement, but if I were to leave London forever, I would have few regrets."

He smiled gently. "Where would you like to make your home, then?"

"I long to live in the country, where I can hunt and shoot to my heart's content. I would do almost anything to make this London season my last." Not that she would marry, of course. That was rather too steep a price to pay for the prospect of ending one's seasons. Besides, if she had a daughter, she would be forced back to London in sixteen years as a chaperone. Louisa-Margaretta, who hated the very thought of motherhood, saw such an eventuality as a rather cruel punishment.

"You do not wish for anything from your life apart from good hunting?" he asked.

Louisa-Margaretta, who had not had many conversations with Mr Fudge during the past year, could not tell whether he mocked her. But she did know that he was a kind listener, which meant she could be open with him in a way that she would not have dared with most gentlemen. "What else am I permitted to expect from life?" she asked. "A profession, for me, would mean the end of all social standing. So I am to live under the roof of my parents, brothers, or husband. It seems to me I ought to at least have a roof that does not leak."

There was little conversation after that, and it seemed that Mr Fudge was still blinking in surprise when she finally left him. She searched for Lavinia, hoping that she and her friend could at least take shelter while partaking of the rather disgusting refreshments.

But she encountered only her mother, who was also searching for Lavinia.

And the mission she had in mind was a much more dramatic one.

"Louisa-Margaretta," she said. "Think quickly. Have you seen Lavinia?"

The rumours were flying through the room already. Louisa-Margaretta saw person after person turn toward a partner, whispering with an intent look on their faces.

"She probably found it rather dull and went home."

Sherborne was standing with a man in a very fine set of clothes. Both of them were scanning the room, neither looking happy. Sherborne had pursed lips and pale skin, and his friend seemed to be almost swaying.

"Louisa-Margaretta," said Mama again, and she shook her head.

"You can call on her tomorrow, Mama," she said. "Is there anything decent to eat tonight? I suppose there is not, but I am very hungry."

Mrs Haddington was the mother of many children. The boys had come first, then Louisa-Margaretta, who was less obedient than any of her brothers. As such, it was rare for Mrs Haddington to become truly angry.

But there was fire in her voice when she spoke to her daughter again. "I do not ask for my own amusement," she said. Beneath the anger, Louisa-Margaretta was surprised to hear a note of fear.

"They found some of her things," said Mrs Haddington. "I am afraid it looks as if something may have happened to her. So I will not ask more than once. When did you see her?"

Underneath her mother's words, Louisa-Margaretta pieced together the story. She was not such an innocent as to be ignorant of the ugliness of the attacks that happened on women. *But not in Almack's, surely?*

"I have not seen her for ages. Just once, across the room, when we came in. But she cannot be far."

Sherborne had reached them. "We must leave," he said, his voice quavering.

Louisa-Margaretta noticed that his well-dressed friend seemed to have disappeared.

"Mama," he said. "They are calling in those Bow Street Runners. Please, let us leave."

8

The men from Bow Street came the first day. The gossip was all over London, of course, speculating that a young woman had been killed at Almack's. Dorothy was so callous as to say that if it were true, it would show up the ladies who guarded the gates of Almack's so closely, though Mr Haddington's reprimand of her was uncharacteristically harsh.

"A young woman may have come to harm," he said. "Must not our thoughts go only to her safety and the suffering of her family?"

Dorothy was heartily ashamed but proud enough not to show the family. And her brother hardly fared better. Jasper was shut up in the family's small sitting room with two men from Bow Street for the better part of an hour. When Judith entered after, he spoke to her in a voice hollow from barely suppressed fear.

"I never thought it would harm anyone," he said. "It was only a joke, one that Sherry and I thought wouldn't do any harm."

"What was only a joke?" Judith asked.

"I went to Almack's," he said just as his parents entered.

And the subject was finished between them for a day, as they were never again together. Judith felt a kernel of pride at being the only person her cousin trusted with the secret, as with his parents, he insisted that he was interviewed only because he was acquainted with a very close friend of the missing young woman.

The next day, a man came who was much older than the young men who had been tasked with speaking to Jasper at first. He introduced himself as Mr Christmas Fudge, the magistrate. His accent placed him on a higher social rung. He did not need the income his position as a magistrate provided and had hired the men so disparagingly referred to as "Bow Street Runners" by the rest of London.

Judith did not hear their conversation, as her aunt had taken to her bed with weeping. Judith's mother immediately provided a sympathetic ear to her sister-in-law, and so it fell to Judith to comfort Dorothy.

Dorothy, however, did not appear to have taken her uncle's words to heart. Her chief complaint was that Jasper always received more of the family's attention, and her mother would never have wept so over one of her transgressions.

"I am sure she would be most unhappy, were you to be in any trouble with the law," ventured Judith, staring out the window as if the solution to their predicament might be found in the busy street below.

"She would hardly take any notice of me," said Dorothy. "Well, she is so cross at least she will not forbid me anything. Let us go have some fun, the two of us! Would your mother allow us to go to Vauxhall, do you think? There is a very dull lady in our neighbourhood who might lend us her maid as a chaperone."

"There is nobody from your own household who would suit?" asked Judith.

"Goodness, no. There is only Mary, but she is frightfully strict when mother is not with me. We should not be permitted even to speak with a gentleman, not a friend of long standing who happens to be there, and certainly no introductions would be permitted."

That sounded rather perfect to Judith, but she did not know how to refuse. "Well, we can ask, I suppose."

"Do," said Dorothy. "I shall go mad if I remain in this house one moment longer."

Note: For a free and complete copy of this prequel novella, join our newsletter here.

www.ingramcontent.com/pod-product-compliance
Lightning Source LLC
Chambersburg PA
CBHW031031310726
48969CB00007B/1940